Frigid Summer

J. Carie Ann Burton

"Life shrinks or expands in proportion to one's courage." — Anaïs Nin

J. Carie-Ann Burton

DEDICATION

In loving memory of our dear mother

MRS. JANET GREENE JOSIAH

(1948-2009)

We miss you dearly

J. Carie-Ann Burton

ACKNOWLEDGMENTS

I am truly grateful to God for blessing me with this talent. I am thankful that He gave me the ability to put words on paper and bring them to life through this medium. I am also thankful that he has surrounded me with supportive family and friends. To my three awesome children, Mahli, Sage, and Dylan, I am very proud to be your mother – thank you so much for constantly crowning me as 'The Best Mommy Ever' and for understanding when I needed some 'me time'. I love you all soooo much! To my best friend – for encouraging, pushing, critiquing, and for all the hard work you put in so that I could see this project come to fruition. Without your support I'm lost! To my brothers – her presence is felt every day! Love you both. To my readers, thank you for your support, I appreciate you all...keep watch...there is more to come.

J. Carie-Ann Burton

CHAPTER ONE

Warm liquid splashed onto my back, it burned as it trickled into the scrapes, cuts and bruises I had gotten from being dragged and pushed on the dry twigs and branches. The pieces that had been discarded by the trees, now contributed to the scarring of my skin. They dragged me like an old rag doll, not caring that my bare arms and legs connected with every object they rubbed against. Every jagged edge drew blood. The liquid ran down my neck and settled into the spot on the ground where my face was eventually planted. They had finally found a place they thought was good enough to continue with their torturous actions. The warm liquid smelled like urine; as the smell grew stronger I became more certain that it was. There was no mistaking the pungent odor. I bit down hard on a piece of stick I had managed to scoop between my teeth; my lips were bruised by its roughness when I moved my face in an effort to keep the liquid from filling up my nose.

The pain that rocked my entire body was intense. A pair of hands lifted the lower part of my body and then dropped it. My face remained buried in damp moss, dried leaves, and dirt. The combination of the strong smells made it almost impossible to breathe. The pressure in my chest was a sensation I had never felt before. I tried to control my breathing, I willed all my strength to lay as still as possible even though my lungs burned with each breath. I had heard them say that if I moved or tried to run again, they would kill me. I did not want to die!

I could taste my blood as I bit harder on the stick. I tried to take deep breaths but that grew more difficult. I forced myself and took one at a time; one in and one out. I continued to put pressure on the piece of stick that was still between my teeth. I kept that as my focus because it was better than me having to pay attention to what was happening to me at that time. At least the bite was controlled by my own actions; I could press down with my teeth as hard as I wanted, they did not control that. There was another thud and I felt a sharp pain; something cracked. I had received another kick to my side; my ribcage burned fiercely.

They laughed, spat, and stomped. This was fun for them; beating, kicking, and raping me were all a part of their sick game. Whatever *evil* had driven them to do this was in full effect. I was slapped when one tried to put his lips on mine and I resisted. Practically numb and surely swollen, the thought of one of them putting his mouth on mine, made me want to vomit. I was punched in the face again, I felt dizzy and started to shake. A flash of bright light appeared when the blow connected. I mustered up some strength, just enough to help me blink a few times. The light vanished and the pounding in my head slowed to a steadier beat.

Time crept on and their wicked game continued. The poking and prodding, the sexual abuse, the hitting – punches to the body and slaps to the face. It was clear that pummeling my body was fun for them. Obviously my life was worth less than theirs' so it was ok to destroy it; I was nothing to them. I endured the attack for several more minutes. I was raped over and over again. As they violated me, they laughed and jeered. I fell in and out of consciousness and eventually lost count of the number of times this cycle happened.

Unexpectedly, the beating and the rape stopped then there was scary silence. I thought they were exhausted or couldn't think of anything else to do to me. I remained motionless; determined not to give them any reason to start the abuse again. I felt raw, inside and out; the pain was just as intense now as it was when it first began.

Finally, after what seemed like a lifetime of silence, one of them spoke.

"The little stuck up bitch is dead; she's not moving. How about we do her one more time before we leave?"

One of them poked my side and then tried to turn me over. I lay still, holding my breath while struggling to keep the pain from taking over. I knew that I was in bad shape and I waited for the next excruciating wave to return. I was sure my shaking would give me away.

A sickening laugh followed his words, an annoying, sinister sound that only a person without a soul could make. The other one, seeming to speak with some sort of conscience, responded to the suggestion.

"Good God, Eugene, I think she's dead! Are you really gonna have sex with a dead body? Come on man let's get outta here. I think we've done enough."

The words sounded more like a plea than a question or command. That one seemed scared.

The other one replied in a nonchalantly.

"Good if she's dead, then she won't feel my thunder."

His laughter echoed in the woods; an animal's cry responded to the high pitch of sound but soon subsided and then there was silence once more, it only lasted but for a moment.

I waited and I prayed *"please God, make them stop"*. Before my words drifted through the darkness, I felt the strings that were remnants of my underwear being ripped from around my legs, and the force of knees as my thighs were spread apart. He rammed his penis in and out of my vagina; at this point, I just let the tears flow. I didn't care if they knew that I was still alive. I just wanted to die. Death would certainly be better than this hell I was going through.

"Take that you little slut. You like it don't you?"

His thrusts continued to rock my body, my head rubbed hard against the dirt and gravel beneath it.

I accepted that I had no control; they could do whatever they wanted to me. At this point, permanent darkness was all I begged for and my prayer changed to match my surrender. *'Please God, let me die.'*

The same sickening laughter filled the night air and the thrusts continued to come harder and faster. The fire inside me burned like the viciousness of a thousand pyroclastic blasts. My limp body jolted with each move. I screamed inwardly, I begged for death over and over again. Salty tears spilled uncontrollably down my dirt and blood encrusted face. I bit on my bottom lip, the piece of twig I had held on to with my teeth had fallen away. I saw my Momma's beautiful face! My Daddy's soothing voice echoed in the wind!

'*My Princess.*'

'*Daddy please come get me!*' I whispered back. I needed him.

'*Please Daddy; I really don't want to die!*'

My lips barely moved but I hoped that God sent my whisper to him. The image of my mother and the whispers of my father were enough to make me want to cling to life. The wish for death disappeared from my mind.

For whatever reason, the thrusts finally stopped; however, the fire within me continued to burn. More of my tears joined the urine on the damp, musty floor of the woods. I couldn't take another minute of this, I wanted it to be over. I whispered another prayer but just when I thought they were through with me, I received another kick to my side. I came to the resolve that my end was near.

'*Please stop*' I begged silently, '*please, please just stop it.*'

I drifted into darkness again, and this time it took me back to my tenth birthday.

Daddy had taken me to the county fair to celebrate the special occasion. It was wonderful. I rode the roller-coaster, played games and ate my favorite foods – hot dogs, funnel cakes, and popcorn to name a few. The best part of the day was having ice-cream with my Daddy; we sat together and talked about so many different things. Just the two of us; I could ask for nothing more.

The memory seemingly helped to lessen the pain for a moment and my thoughts were all about my Daddy and that beautiful day

CHAPTER TWO

It was a warm summer day! I was very excited because my Daddy was coming to see me. Momma had waited until two days before his arrival to tell me. She did this because whenever I learned that he was coming to visit me, I would talk about it all day and night, getting on the nerves of everyone who would listen to me go on and on about it. This time around was no different; as soon as I found out I was chatting away. I was so happy I didn't know what to do with myself. On the days before Daddy came, I would hardly sleep; that was not an option. How could I allow the Sandman to take me? My thoughts about seeing Daddy and hugging him were stronger than any sleep potion.

When Daddy left for the military I was just a baby, so I didn't have much memory of him when I was a little girl, but as I grew older, I came to appreciate his visits and the time I got to spend with him. At first, his time with me were short because he could only get leave from duty for short periods. After he left the service, he got a job in Virginia where he took up permanent residence. Going back to civilian life freed up more time for him to visit and so we got to be together more often.

With all the anxiety building up over the weeks leading up to my Daddy's visit it seemed impossible for me to think of anything except seeing him. I would sit on the bed staring at every object, thinking of all that I would talk about. The fun I would have just getting all of his attention;

the joy that showed on his face as he listened to all my stories, and laughed at all my jokes were moments I would cherish forever, they meant the world to me.

My eyes darted around the room and finally came to rest on my clothes that were neatly laid out across the chair in my room – well the room I shared with my grandmother. I had chosen my black and white polka dot dress with a white sailor's collar and a board red bow that tied in the back. My well-polished, black leather shoes shone in the moonlight; they were my favorite pair. Momma had given them to me the year before for my 9th birthday. I wore them on special occasions only, and Daddy's visit was certainly worthy of me dressing up. My outfit was a bit fancy for the fair, but I wanted to look my best.

The silver crystal like light from the full moon shone through the thin curtains covering the window. Grams – as I called my grandmother – didn't want to close the shutters; she loved when the moonlight came in. We would play shadow games until we both grew weary, and then I would listen intently as she told me stories about when she was a girl. Sometimes she would tell me things about my mother's childhood, like the story of how my Momma would tell Grams that as soon as she was able to, she would move away. I would laugh at the stories if they were funny or ask questions if I didn't understand the 'lesson' that Grams was trying to teach. Tonight was different though, none of Grams' stories would interest me; I just wanted to see the moon leave, and the sun take its place.

I looked over at where my shoes were once more then back at my clothes; time seemed to be creeping. I gently touched my grandmother to see if she was still asleep. She let out a loud snore and pretended that she was asleep. I giggled, giddy with excitement and also finding Grams' fake snore to be funny as well. My grandmother giggled along with me.

"Grams, you weren't sleeping?" I asked as I turned to face her.

She adjusted the covers and then replied,

"Child, close your eyes, staying up all night won't bring your daddy here any faster."

"I know Grams, but I'm so happy that my Daddy is coming to get me. You know how much I love the time I get to spend with him when he comes. I'm too excited to sleep Grams."

"Uhmm Hmm" was my grandmother's reply.

I twisted and turned a few times until Grams finally told me to lay still and go to sleep. Apparently, I had pulled the covers off her one time too many. I squeezed my eyes tightly, counted to 6 or at least I thought I got to 6, and then finally I let the Sandman work his magic. He sprinkled me with his sleep potion, and I had no choice but to give in.

The next day, as soon as I finished my breakfast and chores, I took a bath and then carefully put on my clothes. I was dressed and ready hours before Daddy was to arrive but I wanted to leave for the fair as after he got there. There was no time to be wasted; every second with him was valuable. Seeing him and being the center of all of his attention was what I looked forward to most.

The hours went by slowly but my Daddy finally drove up to the house. Several times while I waited, both Grams and Momma had to beg me to stop looking out the window; it seemed that I got up and peered out too often. When I tried to move my fidgeting and anxiety to the porch, Grams stepped in and gave me a stern warning.

"As early as it is in the day, its hot and humid little girl. Your father will be here in time, walking around or sweating in this heat will not change his arrival time. Go take one of your books and read; that will pass the time more quickly."

Read? Was Grams really serious? As much as I loved

my books today was one day that my focus would be nonexistent. I decided to sit in the living room because the couch was right next to the window. It was the perfect spot to see the car pull up and my Daddy step out.

Momma sat on another chair across from me, her legs were crossed but she shook them nervously. Although she would never admit it, she was just as excited to see my father as I was. A lit cigarette hung from her lips; her left eye squinted as the smoke wafted up and into the air. She took a pull, then removed it from her lips and tapped the middle so that the ashes could fall into an ash tray on the table beside her. Grams always complained about her smoking in the house because it made everything smell of cigarette smoke. If Grams complained enough, Momma would smoke outside for a few days but she would go right back to her old habits soon after.

As far back as I could remember, my mother smoked. At first it didn't really bother me but as I grew older it became more and more of a nuisance. Now, I hated that she smoked so much; she was ruining her body. At times she smoked more than she ate. Cigarettes meant more to her than food; it was a shame, I thought. I begged her to quit and she promised that she would, but every day she continued to fill her lungs with the toxic fumes. I gave up trying.

I watched from the window as Uncle Percy's yellow Thunderbird pulled up. Daddy was alone. He had probably dropped off Uncle Percy at his bar. Uncle Percy's car was always available when Daddy came on visits; it was what he used to get around

As soon as I saw the car, I jumped up from the chair; the excitement had returned with full force. Daddy stepped out of the vehicle, stretched a bit, then he walked up the rickety steps that led to the porch; he was all smiles.

From inside, you could hear the creaking wood of the steps. Uncle Percy had fixed the bottom section of for us about two years or so ago but now, from the sound of it, it was time to get the entire thing repaired. The house needed some painting on the outside as well, but Momma said she couldn't be bothered to see about such things until Christmas. It was an old house, but it had been home to us for as long as I could remember. It had everything we needed, even an indoor bathroom with running water; Momma and Grams had both worked hard to get us that amenity. I loved my house, and I was happy to have it. Daddy's arrival brought more joy to it.

Grams sat on the porch in her rocking chair; she had a basket of green beans on her lap, snapping them as she hummed. It was funny to me that she thought the heat and humidity was too much for me, yet, she found her way and sat there like it was a cool fall day. I believed that she too was anxious to see Daddy but of course she would never say that it was so.

"Afternoon Miss Ida May."

Daddy greeted Grams as he reached the top step and walked on to the porch. He took off his hat as he approached her. My grandmother smiled then waved her hand; she continued with her snapping and humming. Daddy gave her a kiss and a hug, she turned her cheek and grinned. Grams was happy because I was happy, I knew it was so because she had said that to me on many occasions.

"Rae, I am at my best when you are smiling inside and out" she would say to me.

Although he wasn't a constant presence in my life physically, Grams knew that my Daddy and I shared a special bond. I wrote to him all the time, and he did the same. On birthdays I would also receive cards and packages. He kept up with fatherly duties; he knew every milestone that I met at various points in my life so far. There was nothing about my life and my growing up that he wasn't aware of.

I looked over at Momma; she had fixed her hair really nice; it looked shiny and bouncy just like it was in the pictures she had of her younger days. I was impressed. She even had on some make up; the bright red lipstick made her lips look full, and the mascara she wore enhanced her already long lashes. She looked beautiful. Her pink and white candy striped dress had a bow tied to the left side; the style showed off her curvy figure. I remembered the dress, she wore it a few weeks ago when she went to dinner with her friend Beryl. Her social life was limited and prior to the dinner, it had been awhile before that since Momma had gone out.

I could tell that Daddy's breath was taken away. His gaze was fixed on Momma for more than a minute. They both pretended that there was nothing special about seeing each other again. They exchanged pleasantries.

"Hey Edna Jean, you're looking like a vision."

Daddy gave Momma a peck on the cheek and a hug, it was a close hug. She giggled a bit and pretended that she didn't like it by brushing him off when they finally released their grip on each other. The huge grin spoke volumes. In her younger days, Momma was a beautiful and bright young lady. Her beauty turned a lot of heads and caught a lot of eyes. Momma had even entered the Magnolia Pageant held right here in Georgia; a picture of her in her competition eveningwear hung proudly above the bed in her room.

My mother was statuesque; she stood 5'7", her complexion was that of milk chocolate, and equally as smooth. Her smile, although not as bright as before, was still infectious. Her hair was still long and beautiful; the fullness really showed when she let it all out. These days instead of sporting soft curls that lay on her shoulders, she opted to keep her hair mostly in a bun pinned in the back of her head. She claimed that her days of glamour were long gone, but I thought the she had asked those days to leave; it was as if she wanted to forget them. She rarely shared that part of her life with me. Despite all she had been through, I knew that there was still a beautiful woman hidden behind the plumes of cigarette smoke that my Momma blew into the air.

Momma's beautiful brown eyes twinkled; the sparkle grew brighter as she looked at Daddy and replied to his earlier comment.

"Oh hush Ray; you don't know what you talking about."

She lit another cigarette, then blew the smoke into the air. I sighed, she was spoiling the moment. Time, trials and those same darn cigarettes made Momma look much older than her thirty eight years. She could quit if she wanted to, I was so sure of it.

My Daddy's booming voice broke through my thoughts and I instantly forgot about Momma and the smoke.

"Where's my Baby Girl?" He asked.

Daddy squared his shoulders as he uttered those words. He was as proud a papa as one could be. I walked shyly from behind the beads that separated the kitchen from the living room. I had found a spot and stood there watching all this time.

"I'm here Daddy" I said, almost in a whisper.

I was happy and nervous at the same time, I got this same mix of emotions every time. The joy I felt whenever I saw my Daddy always had me acting this way.

"Come here and give your Daddy a hug, Lil Princess."

I mustered up some courage and walked over into my Daddy's arms. He scooped me up effortlessly; his big hug swallowing my small body. I nuzzled my face into his neck. He smelled so good; I would remember the smell for weeks after he left. He kissed and hugged me; I felt like I was in heaven.

My Daddy was a tall man; he stood 6 feet 6 inches and was built like one of those men I would see in the sports type magazines that I looked at with Baby Boy, my neighbor and friend. The men all had huge arms and rigid stomachs. They looked like they could move a 5 story building using their bare hands.

I was on top of the world now, being in my Daddy's arms was the best thing ever. I hugged him tightly and continued to take in his scent. He smelled like old spice and coconut oil. His hair was short and wavy, and he preferred a clean shaven face which felt soft against my cheek. He was dressed in a blue short sleeved shirt that was well starched; it hugged his huge muscles and fit him perfectly. His grey pants had seams as sharp as razors and they fell just right over his shiny, well-polished black leather shoes. He was a good looking man, there was no doubt.

He continued to hug me tightly, I felt safe; no one could harm me, and no one could spoil my joy at that very moment. Nothing else in the world mattered.

"You spoil that girl too much Ray."

I rolled my eyes; not so that Momma could see; that would be disrespectful, and if I got caught a scolding would be sure to follow. I rolled my eyes to the ceiling, so that I was the only one who was aware of what I did. I guess my mother didn't quite know what to say at the moment so she made the comment about Daddy spoiling me. What else could her reasoning be?

It was the same thing Daddy and I did every time he came to visit, he would hug me, and I would wrap my arms around his neck and hang on for as long as he'd let me. That was our thing. Why did she have to say something foolish about him spoiling me? Had she forgotten that I had not seen him in almost 6 months? Didn't I deserve all the attention he could give? How could she consider that as anything but pure love and appreciation for the time I could spend with him?

Growing up with him being far away in the military was one thing and then dealing with the fact that he lived in another state was another. Both were hard to deal with. The long distance relationship with my Daddy more than a girl my age should have to deal with. It was really difficult not having him around'; a little girl needed her father and my mother was well aware.

I let my head rest on Daddy's shoulder for another minute or so, I knew he would put me down eventually but I was taking it all in. He eased me down so that I stood on my feet and then gestured by nodding towards the car that it was time for us to get ready to leave.

"You make sure you don't ruin that dress, you hear me?"

My mother's words faded in the warm summer breeze as I walked speedily through the front door and down the steps. I crossed the small patch of gravel that separated me from the car, I opened the door then hopped onto the back seat. I sat upright and inhaled deeply; Uncle Percy's car smelled good; he kept it clean all the time. The leather seat felt soft against my skin. It was not the first time that I rode in the car, Uncle Percy would drive me and Momma into town or take Grams and me to church any time we needed. This was not a new experience by any means but riding around with Daddy was different from those times.

From Grams' accounts, Uncle Percy and my Daddy grew up together in Georgia. As young men they were inseparable. Uncle Percy was just as tall as Daddy and just as solidly built. Both men could easily pass for brothers, except that Uncle Percy was fairer skinned. His freckles and grey eyes were a magnet for the young ladies; at least that's what Grams said when she told stories about him.

After Daddy and Uncle Percy finished their schooling, they tried to find work in Jessup; it was hard to get anything decent to do at that time, as Grams explained. The choices were limited: dishwasher, factory or farm worker. The young men decided to take the factory jobs, and for a while it was ok doing that sort of work. Reality struck when they found the work to be more than the pay. They sought an alternative and the military came calling. With not much options to choose from, they decided to join and as with almost everything else, my Daddy and Uncle Percy became military service men together.

Daddy and Uncle Percy served their country well, and traveled to different parts of the world; they re-enlisted twice making sure to return to Jessup as often as US Marine Corps would allow. They were like superstars any time they came home; all the women would flock to the bar where the military men hung out, and try to give them an *extra warm welcome*. Grams never really told me what that meant. I just figured then that it meant they got lots of hugs, but of course, I know better now.

There were so many stories about my parents that I heard from Grams, that sometimes I would get them all mixed up. She loved sharing stories about the young people of back then – especially stories about Momma and Daddy.

Grams would say, "Hmm Hmm, child, your Momma would sneak off in the night and come back here smelling like cigarettes and cheap perfume."

She would slap her knee as she laughed, and I would laugh too, sometimes not quite sure what Grams found so funny.

All that was just a memory for me, and it didn't really matter right now, I was anxiously waiting for Daddy to take me on our fun filled outing. I kept looking at the front door of the house, waiting for him to step out and get into the car.

Daddy chatted with Momma for about 5 minutes before he finally made his way to the car.

"See you soon Grams" I called out to my grandmother; she was still sitting on the porch. She smiled and shook her head.

Daddy got into the car and turned on the engine and the radio began to play. The sounds of the Supremes blasted through the speakers. It was a beautiful day.

Momma stood at the door. She waved at me smiling also as she shook her head also. I knew that she was happy for me, and for herself. She loved my Daddy and he loved her, I was sure of it. I wondered why they didn't just get married, and live together. Their relationship was something I didn't understand at that time. It was a subject that Momma never had time to talk about. She would brush me off by changing the subject every time I tried to ask.

Daddy and I drove down the dusty road leading from my house and then turned on to the main highway that led into town. Our outing was on the way, and my excitement could hardly be contained.

We drove past my friend and classmate Ruth; she and her sisters were playing jump rope in the yard in the front of their house. Ruth was turning the rope with one hand, and had her thumb from the other hand stuck in her mouth. Her front teeth bore the evidence that she had been sucking her thumb for years; they were what we called "buck teeth." Sometimes some of the stupid boys in school would call her "Buck Teeth Ruthie".

The name calling didn't seem to bother her as much as it did me. I was always there to defend her. I tried to discourage her from sucking her thumb, I begged her to give up sucking the thing but she would say that her thumb was her comfort or that it helped her to concentrate. Just like my mother and the cigarette smoking, I gave up trying; big girl like that who still sucked her thumb. I thought it was a mighty shame. If she continued, she would not be able to close her mouth. Those teeth protruded more and more each month it seemed.

Ruth's house was not far from mine; the walking distance was about 5 minutes or so. We traveled home from school together on Mondays and Fridays. On the other days, one of Ruth's sisters stayed for extra lessons and Ruth would wait for her.

I poked my head out of the car so that the girls could see me. When Ruth recognize me, she took her thumb from her mouth and waved excitedly. I shook my head at the thumb sucking part, but waved as I yelled out her name.

"Get your head back in this car, young lady. You'd better be careful; hanging out the window like that is dangerous and Daddy wouldn't want anything happening to his Lil Princess".

I pulled my head back into the car and pretended to be upset. I pouted my lips just far out enough so that Daddy could see. He glanced over at me and laughed.

"Your Mama is right; you sure are a spoiled little girl."

I looked over at him and smiled, I had nothing to say; there was no 'come-back' for his statement because it was true. Daddy's request made me sit back and rest my hands on my lap. My pouting was soon forgotten and I took in the scenery as we made our way to the fair.

Our route took us through the downtown area of Jessup. People filled the streets, hustling and bustling as they went about their business. The windows of the car were down and the slight breeze felt good as it flowed through the vehicle. I turned my face just a little to the left, so that the warmth of the sun could kiss my cheek; I liked the feeling. I smiled inwardly; I truly felt like a princess.

I looked right, then left, and watched the people walking about. None was more important than me at that moment. I pretended that I was the Princess of Jessup, and the people bustling about were my subjects. Uncle Percy's car was my chariot, and Daddy was my driver. I waved at no one in particular, but thought the gesture suited the scene that was playing out in my head. It felt good to be the center of the imaginary attention, and I giggled with delight. Daddy just chuckled along, not sure of what exactly I was doing, but he knew that my wild imagination was on full throttle; he could tell from the look on my face. We both laughed out. The pretend 'royal travel' went on until we arrived at the venue.

The fair was located on the outskirts of town. The tents, rides, and booths were set up in a field where the school football team sometimes practiced and also played games. When the school had special sporting events, and other activities of the sort, they were held here as well.

Sometimes, after school or on weekends I would come to the field with Ruth to watch the football team play or practice. Some of the boys would try to speak to us, but they always smelled like sweat and stinky feet at the end of practice sessions; we pretended we didn't want to give them any attention.

My Daddy maneuvered the car into a parking spot, then got out and came around to open the door for me. I hooked his arm with pride as we walked to the fair entrance. It felt like everyone was staring at us. The joyful sounds of screams and laughter echoed in the air; people were having fun, and the weather was suited to do just that.

At the gate, Daddy bought enough tickets for me to try *all* the rides and to play as many games as I wanted; that meant that I would be well occupied.

"You run along and have fun Princess, Daddy will be right over there" he pointed to the hot dog stand where some other men were standing; a few recognized him and shouted out his name. He waved at them.

Daddy was not one to ride on a roller coasters; Momma would certainly have gone with me if she was here; she enjoyed them as much as I did. I wasn't upset that Daddy chose to stay on the ground, I would have fun the rides anyway. I much preferred that rather than to hear him tell me this or that ride looked too dangerous. I happily took a few of the tickets and I left the rest with him, I was afraid that I would lose them. The rides were fast and high and there was no telling what would happen once I got on the huge spinning machine. There was the possibility that I would spread my arms and scream and the tickets would fall out that way.   That all sounded good in my head but the real reason I left didn't take all of the tickets was because I wanted to keep going to my Daddy.

I walked around for a while then decided to play a few games before going on any of the rides. I soon got bored and decided to ride the Ferris wheel; I ended up riding it twice. I was soon tired of that too and came to the conclusion that it was no fun doing any of it by myself. I looked around for something else to do, something other than games or rides. The only other thing to do was to get something to eat and I wasn't in the mood for that either. I realized that I was not having such a good time anymore.

I looked around to see if any of my friends had come out to the fair. Besides Ruth, I only spoke to Melba and Ella; all the other girls in class got on my nerves. The others actually spoke badly about me and my looks, so I refused to speak to any of them. They never said anything to me directly, but I had heard from others at school that they did.   The stupid cheerleading crew is what I called them: Beatrice, Joy Lyn, and Jemma.   They were pretty girls who only worried about what ribbon to tie in their processed hair or what color panties to wear so the nasty football boys could see when they did their cheers and lifts; I hated them! I snickered to myself and then I looked over to make sure that Daddy was still in the same spot where he was before. To be honest, I secretly wished that those same girls were around, at least I would have something to do besides checking to see where Daddy was.

I looked around to see if the girls were in the crowds. Joy Lyn and Jemma were twins; their mother was the child of a white man, that's what I heard Grams say to my Momma. Grams had history on practically everyone in our small neighborhood. One of the girls was fair skinned like her their mother, and the other was brown skinned like cinnamon. Both had wild bushy hair; I liked their hair but would never admit it to them; they were already full of themselves, and I didn't want to ever say anything *nice* to them. Beatrice, the one who followed them around and pretended she was the one to make them triplet, was brown skinned, smooth as chocolate, and had a smile that could melt a seventy-five foot glacier in less than 5 minutes.

Sometimes I would smile in the mirror; grin my teeth and try my best to mimic Beatrice's smile. It never worked. I hated her, I hated them all! I could never look like them. My hair was too thick like Momma's, and unruly; it did not have the big curly waves like Joy Lyn's or Jemma's; I wore it in two puffs or out wild at times; depending on my mood.

Alone with my thoughts, I looked at my skin; a mocha combination of Momma's and Daddy's complexion. I wished, at times, that I was the same color as Grams; she was fairer than Momma; just so I could at least have something that could make me one of *'the girls'* - if I chose to be.

I shook the thought out of wanting them here from my head. I didn't care about those girls anyway; they were just a bunch of fools. Boys, boys, that was all they spoke about, and I had no interest in any of that. I much preferred to be by myself – for now anyway.

I looked around the grounds at the Fair, using my hand to shade my eyes from the glare of the sun. I spotted Melba and her brothers standing in line at the dunk tank; I ran over to them.

"Raenelle!"

Melba screamed when she saw me.

"You lookin' pretty Rae, your Momma did your hair?"

Melba touched the ribbon and patted my puff.

"Nah, Momma can't do hair Mel, I told you that already." We both giggled.

It was a question she had asked a million times, and each time I gave her the same answer. I stayed with Melba for a while, riding the Ferris wheel again; it was more fun this time. We played some games, and I even gave her some of my tickets so that she and her brothers could ride the Spinning Wheel and go on the Death Drop. I didn't mind sharing one bit. Besides, I had more than enough tickets, and surely would not use them all. The afternoon wore on and we enjoyed the time for a while. I eventually decided that I needed to find my Daddy. I said goodbye to Mel and her brothers then searched through the crowd at the food stand. I spotted him still standing at the same spot, only this time some woman was leaning on him, touching his arms and carrying on. I waved again to Melba and her brothers, then marched over to where my Daddy and the woman stood.

"Daddy can we go get ice-cream?"

I folded my arms and tapped my feet, not caring if the woman was talking to him or not. She could just disappear for all I care. My Daddy came here to be with me, not this...this person – whoever she was.

"Princess you run on now and get some ice-cream."

Daddy reached into his pockets and gave me four quarters.
He was trying to get rid of me. I was having none of that.

"Daddy come with me; today is our day. Don't you want some ice cream too? We can both get vanilla. Come on please Daddy?"

I moved closer so I was right next to him, almost touching the stranger. I looked at the woman, I never saw her around these parts before. Maybe she travelled with the fair; I certainly didn't know her. I didn't care who she was anyway, she was trespassing, and he was my Daddy! I batted my eyes and did my most begging, pitiful look; and he fell for it.

"Ok Princess, we'll get ice-cream together."

Daddy patted my head.

He whispered something inaudible to the woman. She giggled like a child, ran her fingers across his chest then walked away.

"She your friend Daddy? Why she need to be so close to you? She goin' be waiting for you?"

I asked all of these questions as we made our way through the crowd, I didn't care that I was breaking the rules of good grammar with my speech. I was mad!

"Aww, don't you worry your pretty little head about that Princess; she is just a friend."

I accepted his explanation and held his hand tighter. I loved him so much. My only wish right now was that he would stay in Jessup permanently.

We both ordered vanilla ice-cream on small cake cones, the lady serving piled the ice cream on the cone, all the while showing her teeth to Daddy. I was pretty sure that we got more than would normally be served for a small sized order. I folded my arms and waited for her to realize that the cone was about to overflow. She caught it just before the ice-cream leaned over and spilled out onto the ground.

I giggled; Daddy smiled at the young lady, tipped his hat, and then walked away from the booth. We found an area where picnic tables and benches were set up. I licked my ice-cream with precision; doing it slowly because I didn't want it to finish too quickly. I wished this moment in time could last forever, just me and my Daddy having ice-cream.

Daddy looked at me, and smiled.

"You're growing up to be a fine young lady Princess, I hope you're paying attention to your school lessons."

He brushed a light-bug from his face.

The sun was beginning to go down, and bugs were starting to look for bright lights to follow.

"I do my school work Daddy, I always get good grades, and I'm at the top of the class. I always am, ask Momma."

I answered confidently, it was the truth.

"I know Princess, she tells me every chance she gets. Your mother is proud of you, and so am I. Enjoy your ice-cream Baby Girl; it's getting dark, almost time for us to get going. Uncle Percy says he has a date tonight and he needs his car back by 8."

We both laughed at the thought of Uncle Percy and his dates. Uncle Percy rarely went on dates; he said that his perfect woman was not in Jessup. I wondered where he thought he would find her if he didn't go looking?

I looked proudly at my Daddy, he was a big and powerful man. I felt protected now that he was here with me. I felt loved, and I truly felt like *royalty*. People stared at him when he walked by, and my being with him meant that they noticed me too. I wanted him to be there when I woke up in the mornings; I needed to know that I would see his face every day. But he lived in Virginia, working as he said, to make life better for me. My Life would already be better if he was around all the time. I sensed that it was something with him and Momma though.

I really enjoyed all the beautiful moments with my Daddy. He looked at me again with a twinkle in his eyes. I knew that he loved me, I was his Princess!

CHAPTER THREE

Mr. Smooth and His Band worked their magic on the crowd at the Midnight Blues Club. Mr. Smooth's sexy way of bringing his instrument to life drew crowds. The women licked their lips when he placed his mouth on the saxophone and blew; and boy could he blow. They envisioned themselves as his sax, making beautiful melodious notes come to life as he caressed and blew.

The hypnotic sounds that flowed from the sax created a matrimonial union with the instruments of his band members' as they harmonized bass, piano and drums. The combination was perfectly in sync. Mr. Smooth was a musical genius. Friday and Saturday nights were busy at the Midnight Blues Club; Mr. Smooth and His Band drew crowds as the main attraction.

Kenton Franks, also-known-as Mr. Smooth was a handsome Mulatto with a smile that melted hearts. His honey complexion, soft curls, goatee and piercing green eyes mesmerized all women – both young and old. These same women rushed to the front of the stage when Mr. Smooth and His Band was introduced by the MC; the women screamed and threw things – panties included – but he played it cool at all times; he was used to that sort of thing

He commanded and received attention when he walked on stage. Always looking and smelling so good. Women screamed his name, begged him to marry them, and offered to have his babies. He responded to all these requests by blowing his sax, using the instrument to give his audience the opportunity to enjoy the sweet sound of Jazz. He blew kisses, winked, or flashed a smile to keep the momentum of the salivating women going. As part of his routine, he would pick a lady from the crowd at random and invite her onstage, twirl her around and then serenade her. This would drive the other women in the crowd crazy. They would scream louder as he pressed his body close to the 'lucky' woman. He would whisper sweet nothings into her ears and she would stare at him – star-struck. Mr. Smooth was very good at what he did and he never disappointed. The woman would leave the stage with wobbly feet; a symptom of being bit by the *bug*; that was a clear sign that she now had the *Smooth Fever*.

From a dark corner in the back, Edna smiled, she enjoyed being at the Midnight Blues Club. She loved to watch the women scream for a man they would never have, or at least not for more than one night. There were rumors that Mr. Smooth would bed one or two of his 'picks', but there were no confirmations, so it remained just that – rumors. It amazed Edna to see how one man have such an effect on so many women. True, Mr. Smooth was a looker, his eyes were hypnotizing and he sure knew how to blow a saxophone, but all of that could not compare to her man.

Ray, hmmm, just the thought of him sent shivers down her spine. He was perfect, cinnamon toned smooth skin, 6 feet 6 inches tall, and the body of a Greek god. She felt her heart race and a tingling between her legs as his image popped into her head; she put on thigh on the other and squeezed. Smiling, she closed her eyes and remembered how good it felt to be wrapped in his arms, his muscles huge and bulging felt good. With or without clothes, his body was a beautiful thing. She loved her man; he was hers and she was his; they were meant to be together.

~~~~~~~~

Ray and Edna were both natives of Jessup, Georgia. Born and raised in the same neighborhood they shared similar childhoods, they were a part of the same circles, from attending school, church, to the sharing of friends. Their mothers worked at the same nursing facility and both women were of the same strict Baptist faith. They attended church every Sunday, and at nights too if there was a crusade or other activity; and made sure that their children were present at all times.

As they grew older, Ray and Edna began to look forward to the church events because it meant they could see each other outside of school. They never thought of themselves as anything other than good friends, although eventually they both accepted that there was more to their relationship than just being *close* neighbors. Whatever *it* was, the relationship gradually developed over time. At school events Edna made sure that she was the girl sitting next to Ray. At the end of the school day, other boy had the opportunity to carry her books home. Ray made sure that he was at the exit to meet her before anyone else had the opportunity to ask. It came as no surprise to anyone when they officially declared themselves as a couple. Ray asked Edna to be his girl on the day of high school graduation when he asked her to be his prom date. From that moment onward they became even more inseparable.

Edna's thoughts returned to present. Mr. Smooth and His band finished the first set and announced that they would be taking a short break. The women moaned with displeasure as they dispersed and returned to their tables. Their disappointment lasted but for a moment, soon drinks were served and a thousand different conversations filled the air. The mixture of voices and clinging glasses began overpowering the music coming from the jukebox, a few couples rocked to the beat in dark corners of the smoke filled room. Women were at the club solo mingled, and men of the same kind tried their best to charm them. Edna watched the action from her seat, she recognized a few of her old school mates as she looked around in search of Ray. She suddenly realized that he had been gone for a while.

She was still looking about the room when she felt a hand on her shoulder, she knew his touch; it still sent waves throughout her entire body; she smiled. She placed her hand over his; he kissed the back of her neck, then came around and sat in the chair next to her. The sound of Otis Redding's 'You Made a Man Out of Me' reached them from the jukebox. Ray playfully snapped his fingers and began to sing along.

"Let's dance Baby."

He took her hand.

Edna smiled at her man as she stood up and walked over and held him close; he continued to sing. They danced right next to the table; perhaps they would go onto the dance floor when the band returned but dancing right here was just as good. It felt wonderful to be loved and to be in love. When the song was over, Ray stopped his rendition as well, and helped Edna to her seat.

"You haven't finished your drink yet Sugar."

He looked at the glass sitting on the table. The pale liquid had lost its original dark brown color, the ice had watered it down.

"I was waiting on you; I wanted to make a toast Baby but you were gone for so long."

Edna batted her lashes; she pouted her full lips and pretended to be upset.

"You disappeared for a while. I was beginning to think that someone had stolen you from me".

He chuckled. "I'll make it up to you Sugar, I saw some fellas I haven't seen in a long time; we were chit-chatting for a few. Nobody can hold a candle to you Baby. Steal me away? Never!"
He planted a kiss on her hand.

Ray signaled to one of the waitress who hurried over to their table. The young woman's gaze was transfixed on him as soon as she was close enough to get a good look. She grinned and giggled. Edna was used to this reaction from women; it didn't bother her one bit, after all what woman wouldn't want to get close to this good looking man? She felt proud that she was lucky enough to have him. Ray ordered their drinks, scotch on the rocks for him and cherry cola for his lady; she was not a drinker of alcoholic beverages; a glass of wine on occasions but those were few and far between.

Edna took Ray's hand and played with his fingers; she was so in love with him. Ray returned her playful gesture by raising her hand to his lips and kissing it gently again. His warm breath on her skin set her insides on fire. She couldn't control it even if she tried.

Ray held her gaze. Her beautiful and piercing hazel eyes with thick lashes were enchanting; he felt he could see through to the depths of her soul they were that hypnotic. She was a beautiful woman in every sense of the word. A true Southern queen; in addition to her eyes, she had milk chocolate skin, a body with curves in all the right places and beautiful, curly hair that fell just past her shoulders. She stood at 5'5", but her personality made her seem taller at times. Her words flowed freely; she said what was on her mind, no pretense and no sugar coating. If you wanted to get an open and honest opinion about anything, Edna was more than ready to give.

Ray loved her all the same. She was his woman and he was her man. No other woman could take her place, many had tried and failed and some still do. Drinking in her beauty and looking at her smile at him from across the table, Ray wondered how she was not crowned Miss Magnolia 5 years ago when she entered. Everyone knew that there was no competition; the other ladies paled in comparison to his Edna. For him, she had captured the crown just like she had done his heart years ago. There was nothing in the world that he would not do for her.

About 20 minutes had elapsed and they were still waiting on the drink order. Ray looked about for the waitress, she was sure taking her own sweet time, but he realizes that the club was packed, and getting to the bar was a task in itself. He decided to patient a few minutes He continued longer and looked at Edna sitting at the table. He started to crave her touch, he wished that he could have her at that very moment.

The grinning waitress finally returned with their drinks. She placed a coaster on the table and put the glass filled with ice and cola in front of Edna. A cellophane covered straw was placed next to the glass. Edna picked up the straw and removed it from the wrapper; ice cubes clinked as she stirred the caramel colored bubbly liquid. She took a sip, the bubbles tickled, she closed her eyes and giggled.

The waitress had stated a conversation with Ray, telling him of the appetizers that were still available from the kitchen. Ray thanked the smiling girl whose grin became wider when he placed a few dollars on her serving tray. She took the bills, folded them and quickly pushed them in her bra where she stashed the rest of the tips she had collected throughout the night. She sashayed over to another table to serve her other customers, right after turning to give Ray a wink. Edna laughed out loudly, as did Ray.

Mr. Smooth and His Band returned to the stage, they began to play a soft tune; setting the mood for the final few hours of their act. Slow, romantic notes flowed from the instruments; the mixture of melodies creating fireworks invisible to the eyes. The music commanded individuals to hold each other close and allow the beat to guide their motions; two bodies would easily melt into one.

The band continued to do its thing; Mr. Smooth let his saxophone put a spell on the patrons, only a small space was left on the dance floor. Ray did not want the mood to pass him and his lady by. He took Edna's hand and led her to the center of the room. Several other couples had already gotten there before them, so they made the small space work to their advantage. Tight grips and slow motions took them to another place. The sweet sounds of jazz caressed the bodies that filled the tiny area; the dancers swayed in unison to the beat. Ray pulled Edna even closer. She her head fall onto his chest; he let his cheek rest against her head; her hair smelled like jasmine. Her body melted into his; she felt good in his arms.

As they danced, he relaxed his mind and thought about the perfect time to choose to tell her his news. Tonight, at some point he would have to do it. He had made the decision earlier that day. He had not gotten the job as supervisor at the factory. He had hoped that they would have given him the opportunity; it would've meant that he could ask Edna to marry him. More money would afford him the ability to support her while she pursued her teaching degree. It was her passion and drive to teach, something she spoke about all the time. He wanted that for her more than he wanted anything for himself. To his utter disappointment, they had given the position to someone else.

They came up with some lame reason that although he knew the job inside out, he lacked the credentials to move into that position. Ray knew that it was all bullshit! It didn't matter to them that he had worked there since his high school days; it meant nothing that when someone didn't show up that he took on that person's responsibilities in addition to his own. He outperformed the other employees at every task. None of that mattered to the idiots that ran the factory!

'...didn't have the credentials, pure rubbish!'

He was more certain now that he had to get out of Jessup, he felt stifled, kept back. He'd had enough disappointments as far as his employment status was concerned. He could not support Edna as a man by being an ordinary factory worker. He wanted more for her and for himself as well. He was ready to move on to bigger and better things, which were out there somewhere, just waiting for him to go grab them. Now was his time! No more waiting around for the perfect opportunity that would never come.

He brushed all negative thoughts from his mind; the disappointment, the anger, the frustration; at this moment he only wanted to hold on to his woman. He allowed himself to get lost in her sweet caress, her smell, her smile, and her body. He bent down and kissed her cheek softly.

~~~~~~~~

Edna liked the feeling of being wrapped up in Ray's arms, dancing slowly to the sweet music. She let him lead; she didn't mind following his movements. This was all she needed right now. Her man holding her, making her feel safe and secure. Tonight she would tell him; tonight after they made sweet love, she would give him big the news. She was bursting to tell him; it took all her strength to contain herself the entire time they were together tonight. News like this could not be held in for too long; she had no choice really. A crowded blues club was no place to share this sort of news; she would wait for the perfect setting.

Suddenly she remembered that Ray had had an interview with the manager at the factory for the supervisory position. She was sure that it was just a formality, because Ray was already performing duties pertaining to that role – nothing to it; it was already *in the bag.* She was sure he was waiting for right time to give her his good news; they would make each other happy tonight. His promotion and their addition!

Life wasn't so bad after all. Their future looked good.

~~~~~~~~

Percy rubbed the sleep from his eyes; the pounding on the door woke him from sleep and cut short his glorious dream. Lolita was about to lower her dark luscious body onto his, damn! Sweet Lolita, she came to him in in all her splendor on many nights. She always left him happy with curling toes and all, oh yeah! Lolita, Lolita! Tonight there would be no happy ending for him; he knocking interrupted *them*; she probably wouldn't return, she hated to be disturbed.

"This had better be good, waking a man up from such a fantastic episode." Percy shouted out.

He walked to the front door and switched on the dim porch light, he then lifted the curtain that covered the squared glass at the center of the door. The thin material allowed him to see who was there without actually opening the door. He peered though and recognized Ray and Edna. Not surprisingly, they were grinning, kissing and whispering to each other. Percy shook his head; this could only mean one thing - Edna's mother was home and so was Ray's; the next best place was his. He didn't mind one bit, although he pretended to; Ray meant the world to him and so did Edna, by extension. They came here because neither was allowed to do what they were about to under their mothers' roofs.

Percy sucked his teeth with pretend annoyance and then opened the door; he knew that their soft moans and whispers would keep him awake and wishing that he had a woman too. Now that Lolita was gone from his dream he would have trouble falling asleep for sure. Returning to him after *they* had started was not *her* thing; *she* was an all or nothing sort of girl. Sweet Lolita, if only she would manifest herself into a real woman, that would be perfect.

"Hey Percy P."

Edna cooed as she walked past him, she touched his chest. She was drunk with love; it was so obvious it was almost sickening.

"Now I know that you two have homes to go to. What are you doing at my place at this hour? And Ray where is the damned key I gave you months ago? Pounding down my damned door at this hour. You're lucky I don't have to go to work tomorrow 'because for sure y'all asses would be standing outside 'til the sun come up. And if I only had my girl here, there would be no opening of that damn door for sure!" Percy continued with the charade.

Ray just tapped his friend's shoulder, flashed him a smile, and followed Edna to the back of the house. Percy could not help but laugh, he knew that neither of them was paying him any attention or taking him seriously. Truth was Ray had access to Percy's place any time. They were like brothers.

When Percy lost both parents to a horrendous car crash, he was only 17. It was rumored, but never proven, that the car crash was no accident, and that Mr. Phillips, Percy's father, was involved in some illegal stuff that finally caught up with him. It was further stated that he was laundering money for powerful people and was skimming off the top; it was no small change big money was involved.

To this day, Percy never sought to confirm those allegations and he never discovered any hidden stash of money anywhere in the house either. He had focused dealing with the death of both parents at the same time. The grief of losing them was more than any young person should bear. There was no sense in digging up things he had no knowledge of, and he really found no reason to taint his memories of his parents by looking for dirt on his father. He let the rumors die out and carried on with his life.

During that dark period, it was Ray who asked his mother if Percy could stay with them until he was able to handle living on his own. Percy's mother's side of the family was mostly up north in Delaware, but Ray knew that his friend would not want to leave his home state to go live with people he hardly knew. Luckily for Percy, his parents had a house and were smart enough to have a will as well. Percy knew that he'd be ok; he would be orphaned, but not destitute.

After Mrs. Porter and a trusted attorney take care of all the legalities, the house was rented, and Percy moved in with her and Ray. The boys were inseparable from then until now; they were as close as two boys could be without being *blood* brothers. He lived with them until he turned 21, then he moved back into his family home.

Ray and Edna continued on to the back of the house, and to the second bedroom; there Percy had a bed, and a desk and chair. He called it his den.

"An y'all don't be waking me up with your moans and groans either." Percy called out to them as they disappeared.

He chuckled; they paid him no mind. He shut off the light in the hallway, went into his room and put his pillow over his head. He closed his eyes and wished for Lolita to return, they had unfinished business, but the Sandman came with a double dose of *his* potion instead. Lolita was through with him for the night.

~~~~~~~~

In the small room, Edna stripped down to her bra and underwear. It was a hot summer night and beads of sweat started to form across her forehead. She could feel the heat of Ray's breath on her neck; she wasn't sure which was making her dizzier – the heavy breathing or the stuffiness of the room. Ray spun her around and stared into her eyes. He took in her beauty, the smell of her hair, the soft touch of her fingers on his face. There was something different about her; he couldn't quite put his finger on it. Her face glowed in the light of the room. She undressed him slowly, undoing one button of his shirt at a time, all the while staring in his eyes. She held his gaze; she mesmerized him. He cupped her butt, squeezed the roundness and felt his manhood grow inside his pants she felt it too; she looked deeper into his eyes; satisfied that she had achieved the desired results.

"I want you so bad Baby" she whispered.

"You can have me" he whispered back.

"I have something to tell you."

She said between featherlike kisses on his rock solid chest.

"You can tell me anything Sugar."

Ray gently rubbed her nipples; he reached down and put one in his mouth. She took a deep breath, the feeling sent shivers down her spine. She lost her train of thoughts for a moment.

"I have something to tell you too" he said to her.

She gently lifted his head and took him by the hand; they walked over to the bed and sat down.

"You go first" Ray said to her.

She took a deep breath, "I love you Ray Porter."

She played with his fingers, twisted them, and twirled them.

He cupped her face with his free hand.

"Talk to me Sugar; tell me what is on your mind."

She took his hand and placed it on her belly.

A few minutes passed then Edna finally spoke.

"A tiny you and me is growing inside me Ray Porter, you're going to be a Daddy. I'm pregnant."

She giggled. His heart stopped! He let it sink in. He stared blankly for a few more seconds then kissed her on the lips. He swallowed hard; he certainly didn't expect this news. Not that he was upset or anything; he wasn't sure what or how to feel – at least not at this very moment.

A few more seconds had passed then he began to make circular motions on her belly with his hands. It was slightly pouched, the little rise was barely noticeable but she was already showing signs. Her skin gave off a radiance that he had noticed earlier; it all made sense now. She was carrying his seed, his offspring. He would be responsible for this little human being until he or she was able to take care of his or herself, and even then, he vowed to always be a part of their life. He bent down and kissed her skin, she held his head, rubbed his hair, and whispered his name. He accepted the news with joy.

"Tell me what you wanted to say earlier Ray." Edna said softly.

He remained silent; this was not the appropriate time. He caressed her body, kissed and licked her all over until she begged him to make love to her. The mood had changed a bit for Ray, but he did his best to please her, she was hungry for his lips, for his kisses, for his touch, and for the feeling that came when their bodies finally became one. He satisfied her desire but his intensity was not as it usually was; she felt it but said nothing until they lay side by side.

"What's the matter Baby?"

Edna made circles on his chest with her index finger. He pulled her close and kissed her full head of hair, it was wild now after their love making.

"Nothing Sugar, I'm about to become a Daddy, I'm letting it sink in."

Satisfied with his response, she snuggled closer and whispered to her man that she loved him, then drifted off to sleep. Their breathing mixed with the hot night air, the sound of the crickets in the night, and Percy snoring in the room next door. Ray lay awake through to the early hours of the morning.

CHAPTER FOUR

Shadows danced across the water. The moon shone brightly that night, and the glow from its light along with the cool breeze created the perfect atmosphere for a stroll along the banks of the lake. Ray held Edna's hand as they walked barefoot on the grassy area where children played in the daytime and mothers kept close watch as they sat on blankets.

They had come here many times for picnics in their childhood days; they had had many fun times. The lake was not far away from Percy's house; these days they spent more time at their friend's house than ever before. Being there was good for them; they could lay together quietly and talk about their future which now included their *new* baby. Edna looked forward to them being together in their own place as a family. It was all she spoke about. It was not that he did not want the same, Ray's issue was finding a job that paid enough to provide them with a decent living situation.

It was quiet that night, only an occasional splash, perhaps a fish frolicking about in the water, or the hoot of an owl, hidden in plain sight, could be heard.

"Are you tired Baby?"

Ray rubbed Edna's hand and then raised it to his lips. He kissed it. Edna was glowing, she smiled and it rivaled the light shining from the moon.

"I'm ok Ray, your baby is very active tonight though, dancing in my belly as if the sweetest tune is being played."

Ray reached down and touched Edna's protruding belly, it had grown so much over the past few months. The baby moved, creating waves that made Edna draw her breath.

"She's creating her own melody; she's dancing to her own beat" Ray said.

"She?" Edna asked. "How can you be so sure it's a girl?"

"Can't you see how she moves every time she hears her Daddy's voice or when I touch your belly? That's my Little Princess."

They both laughed.

"I am going to spoil her rotten!" Ray said.

"And I don't doubt that" Edna responded.

He was getting used to idea of being a father, Ray was anxious to meet his child. And he felt differently now, his emotions had changed from the night Edna had broken the news to him about the pregnancy. Soon a little person would be calling him Daddy, depending on him to provide and protect them, and he was ready mentally to live up to the task. He was not as scared now; he would be there for his child and his woman, no matter what. His grin widened as pride filled his being.

Since the night at Percy's when he got the life-changing news, Ray picked up more hours at the factory, working hard and saving every dollar he could. He was anxiously preparing for the baby's arrival; he wanted to make sure that his child would have everything he or she needed, it was his responsibility to do this.

He was passed over a second time for the supervisory position, even when it didn't work out for the person *they* had hired for the job over him. The excuses and promises continued, but he kept his focus on his family and their needs above his anger and disappointment.

Nothing about his work load changed, he was still expected to perform duties in the same capacity for the same pay. He desperately needed to find another job. Percy had mentioned the military several times, and each time his reasons for joining seemed even more convincing than the last. Percy was trying again today to make that option more practical than before.

"I can't leave Edna now man, she's about to have our baby!"

They were sitting at a table having lunch in the factory's cafeteria.

"Man, I'm telling you, with the benefits from the Marines, you can take care of Edna and the baby without working in a dump like this for the rest of your life."

Percy took a bite of the tuna sandwich he had purchased, he then took a napkin and wiped the mayonnaise from the corner of his mouth. He chewed as he spoke, a habit Ray found annoying, but he said nothing to his friend.

"Listen man, I have all the information we need at my

place, you can come look them over after work. It's time for us to do something different, not stay around Jessup and work at no damned factory. We are two able bodied young men. It would be great for us Ray, think about it."

Percy threw the napkin in a waste basket and pushed the plate with the other half of his sandwich away from him. He had the look of desperation and despair on his face. He too was tired of the factory work and living in Jessup.

"Alright man, we'll look at the information later on. You know I can't hang around too long though, Edna will be waiting for me." Ray finally replied.

Percy rolled his eyes and waved him away; they both laughed.

Joining the Marines was not the issue; the tough part would be telling Edna of his intention to do so. Ray would have to try his hardest to convince her that it was best for them – the baby included.

CHAPTER FIVE

"I saw her move, she ain't dead."

Those words brought me back to the present. The pain seared through me with a ferocious intensity. I held my breath waiting for the final blow that would take me to the place from where no one ever returned.

"She moved 'cause you were sticking that thing of yours inside her. You a fool Lester! Wasn't you the one who said I was nasty for fucking a dead body?"

Eugene laughed.

"Shit, you make me want to do her again; you were riding her like a race horse."

The same sickening laughter filled the night air.

"Come on man, let's go."

"So we 'gonna just leave her here?"

I lay motionless.

"You wanna take her with us, you fool? Aint nobody gonna find her here; we way off the road. These here woods are filled with wild animals, I'm sure one will find her and eat her ass."

Eugene was talking, I recognized his sickening, annoying high pitched voice.

My heart pounded loudly. I prayed to God that they would not hear my shortened breaths.

"Aw man, com'on Eugene, let's go."

I waited, prayed, and then heard the shuffling sound of footsteps walking away and the cackling laughter as it faded into the night.

The tears stung my swollen eyes and burned the scrapes and bruises on my face as they flowed. I sobbed quietly, for fear that the boys had not left; I did not want them to return for any reason. God help me if they came back and figured out that I was still alive. The night air began to seep through my pores, and there was a chilliness that I felt inside and outside of my battered body, I shivered uncontrollably and every part of my body ached.

After what seemed like an eternity, and when I was sure that the boys had left, I tried desperately to move. I prayed as I slowly began to stir. Between my legs felt sticky, dried blood caked over my left eye, and the right one was totally shut. I grunted as I dragged my hands from my sides and used them to reach the trunk of a tree they had left me close enough to. I painfully dug my nails into the tree and pulled myself closer; my body felt weighted down. I tried to stand; my fingers bled as I dug deeper into the bark of the tree; my ribs hurt, my head pounded, and my legs felt like logs. I had to take a rest, the pain was unbearable. I took short painful gasps of air not knowing if I would make it.

I listened for the sound of the animals that were supposed to come and tear me apart but all I heard was the croaking of frogs, the occasional chipper of crickets, and a distant howling, thank God that there nothing else.

I listened again, I heard cracking twigs, '*oh God no, they were returning*'.

My heart began to pound harder in my chest, and the hammering in my head joined in with force. Instinctively I pulled my body as hard as I could and tried to hide next to the tree trunk. I did used the strength I had left; all the while there flashes of my Daddy, Momma and Grams appeared in my mind. I needed my family; I wanted to cry out for them.

I heard the faint whisper of my name and I trembled with fear.

"Raenelle? You alive there Rae?"

My breath came faster and again I tried to stand.

"It's me, Rae, its Baby Boy. Don't be afraid Rae I won't hurt you."

Baby Boy? What was he doing here? How did he know? I let out a faint cry. He came closer to me and reached out; he began to help me by lifting my battered body. I cried out in pain, howling like a wounded animal when he finally got me up.

"I know who done this to you Rae, I saw them the whole thing."

"Help me Baby Boy" I whimpered. I just wanted to go

home to my Momma.

He stood tall above me and started to remove his suspenders. Was he about to do what I was thinking? Flashes of what happened earlier began to play in my head. Baby Boy moved closer to me. My worst fears were about to come true, Baby Boy was about to do to me what those scum had already done. No, not my friend Baby Boy, he was like my big brother. This could not be!

He took off his shirt exposing his bare chest.

I tried to crawl away but all of my strength had been drained from my body. I leaned against the tree limp, broken, and battered; my legs shook. My life would surely be over this time. *Take me now please God!*

Baby Boy bent down and threw the huge garment over my body. It's warmth came over me and eased my coldness. He had taken off his shirt to cover my body, I just realized that I was practically naked; my clothes had been ripped from my body. He wanted to protect me completely.

My heart rate slowed and I felt warm under the soft material. Baby Boy picked me up gently and carried me through the woods. With every step he took I died a thousand times; the pain of every movement encompassed me, my entire body felt raw – inside and out. It was the most painful journey I'd ever had. When we got to a clearing, Baby Boy stopped, he laid me down on a patch of grass. I was too weak to ask any questions; I just wanted my Momma and Daddy to appear. I needed to be in my house.

"I want to make sure that those boys are not hanging around Rae, hang in there, I won't leave you. I don't trust them two Truitt boys none at all."

Baby Boy left me to look up and down the street, we were close to home. When he was sure that the coast was clear, he picked me up again and made his way to my house. He had rescued me; I would make it home, although I was barely able to move, I was alive nonetheless. It was certain that I would be dead in a matter of hours if he had not found me. I would never have been able to find my way out of those woods on my own, and certainly not in the condition I was left in. Thank God for Baby Boy.

I still desperately wanted to see my Momma.

~~~~~~~~

Baby Boy was 6'9", a huge 20 year old man, with the intelligence of a boy who was 10. He never had the opportunity to finish school; because he was slow in learning, he felt embarrassed and would skip classes. Eventually he just stopped going altogether. I tried to help him learn how to read and write by going at his pace. We would work on the basics every day after I was finished with my school assignments. He would get frustrated with himself easily and fuss about the hard time he had learning. As a result, he was only able to retain a little. He once said that all he wanted was to be able to recognize his name if he saw it. We worked on simple things like that and eventually he was able to read and write a few words as well.

Despite his academic shortcomings, Baby Boy was a warm and caring person – that much everyone knew. I never gave up on him. I made it my business to make lessons out of any activity that I could. Most evenings he would get tired, leave the books and pencils, and chose to sit on the porch with Grams and reminisce instead.

As far back as I could remember, Baby Boy was a part of my life, we practically grew up together. Grams told me that he was a 'menopause baby'. I didn't understand what that meant so she explained it to me. Mrs. Johnson gave birth to Baby Boy when she was 47 years old. He came to her just when she thought that her time to produce any children had long gone. She welcomed her son, Baby Boy was the joy of her. Having someone else to care for besides Mr. Johnson brought her great satisfaction. It had just been the two of them for the first 25 years of marriage. She was happy that he had me as a playmate as well.

Sometimes I would come to Baby Boy's rescue, shielding him from comments made by the likes of Jemma and Joy Lyn. They were the 'popular' girls at school and my self-made enemies. They would make cruel jokes about Baby Boy's mother being old enough to be his grandmother, and they mocked his slow speech and the way he slurred his words when they came out at times. I didn't care about all that because Baby Boy was my friend, and we protected each other.

~~~~~~~~~

Now that he had rescued me from certain death, I made a solemn promise to be there for him even more, and to make sure that he knew that he was loved by me, always. If it weren't for him looking out for me, caring for me like a big brother, I would have surely died in the woods.

Baby Boy gently carried me to the front door; he knocked softly at first then more loudly after a few seconds had passed and no-one had responded. My mother finally peered through the curtains then opened the door. I remembered wondering if she had noticed that I stayed longer than usual to return with her cigarettes.

She looked like she went into shock at the sight of Baby Boy holding me in his arms; bloodied, beaten and limp. She stood and stared for almost a minute, then fell to her knees and let out a long wailing and painful scream. My condition was too much for her to take. When she was able to get up, Baby Boy held my beaten body out to her.

"No God, No No. What happened to her? Who...what...Did you do this?"

In a state of panic and disbelief, my mother tried to grab me from Baby Boy, but she was unable to handle the dead weight of my limp body. She stumbled a bit, then regained her composure and use all of her strength to take me from Baby Boy's arms. Noticing her frantic state, he didn't release his grip but attempted to explain what had happened to me.

"I didn't do this Miss Edna, I found her like this. I would never hurt Rae."

My mother pointed Baby Boy in the direction that led to her room. All the while she continued to stammer and ask what had happened, and demanded to know who had done this thing to me. Baby Boy looked at me and for some reason I shook my head 'no' at him, giving the sign that he was not to tell what he knew. He knitted his brow in a puzzled look but said nothing. He finally reached my mother's room and laid me gently on the bed. My mother's hysteria continued; screaming, pleading, talking in unintelligible hushed tones to me, and then screaming insanely again at Baby Boy.

Grams, on hearing all the commotion, came rushing into the room; she too began to wail when she saw my terrible state.

"Rae, Sweetie, what happened? Who did this to you?" she asked.

Grams turned as white as a ghost; she trembled and

looked around frantically. If I looked half as horrible as I felt, I could understand why they reacted the way they did.

Grams regained her composure a bit, she looked at me lying on the bed; she stared at my blood stained face. She left the room and returned with warm towels and used them to wipe the caked blood and dirt from my face.

"We need to get this child to the hospital or get some real serious help" she said to my mother.

She continued to clean me up. I was numb, cold and shaking; I tried to wrap Baby Boy's shirt tighter around me but that proved too painful and it dropped to the floor. My mother turned to Baby Boy, and between sobs she asked him to go get Dr. Greene. Her face was drenched with tears.

"I'll run get Doc" Baby Boy said.

He took his bloodied shirt from the floor, threw it over his shoulders and sped out of the door.

As Grams continued to clean my face, I lifted my head and tried to speak, I wanted to tell her that I would be ok, but no words came. My lips were swollen and my head was drumming with pain. She wiped my face, careful not to press too hard near my right eye. She then put a cup to my lips and told me to drink, it was water. I sipped slowly and swallowed carefully, my lips were heavy. I still could not open my right eye. I remembered being punched several times on that side of my face. That was what the boys did to me when I fought back. The one named Eugene had slapped and hit me with a force that could only come from anger and hatred. The throbbing in that area of my face reminded me of how severely I was beaten by those bastards!

Grams continued to clean the cuts and scrapes; all the

while my mother stood staring; she had not said much since Baby Boy left. She just cried with her arms wrapped around her waist, and rocked back and forth. The shock had not worn off for her yet.

Baby Boy soon returned; he knocked on the front door, Grams left me to let him in, my mother was too distraught to even move from where she stood. The doctor followed closely behind Baby Boy with his black bag in tow. Dr. Greene was the only doctor in the area that would make house calls to our side of town. He did have a small office in but whenever necessary he would make house calls. This arrangement worked well for the older folks that did not have transportation to travel or were immobile.

Dr. Greene was an elderly white man with skin that resembled beaten leather; he had beady blue eyes, but he was a good doctor. Every one of his patients loved him. He came over and took a look then proceeded to examine me. His hands were rough, perhaps from washing them constantly or perhaps from just being old, and they felt like sandpaper as he touched me. It was meant to be a gentle tap, a slight touch to let me know that he would do his best to take care of me. I relaxed a bit but the pain in my head was still intense.

I was shaking badly by now, I had chills and cold sweat, and I vomited several times over. Grams did all that she could to help me, but my mother only let out deep mournful sighs, and shuddered every now and again.

"What happened to this child?"

The doctor looked suspiciously at Momma, Grams and then back at Baby Boy. Baby Boy stepped forward and spoke.

"I found her in the woods like that Sir, I swear, I found

her that way."

Baby Boy spoke with a frightened look on his face, he stepped back into a corner.

"You folks know that I have to report anything suspicious to the Sherriff, so if there is anything to tell, please do so now."

Dr. Greene surveyed the room once more.

"The boy found her like that Doc, and we believe him; there is no way he would hurt her."

Grams looked at the doctor, and Momma confirmed with a head shake.

My mother had still not said a word.

Satisfied at the moment with what he heard, the doctor proceeded to take a closer look at me. As he began his examination of my beaten body, I tried to focus my fuzzy gaze back to my mother. She still rocked back and forth as she had been doing ever since I was brought in. She looked at Dr. Greene, and watched every move he made.

At some point of the examination, Dr. Greene began to check my swollen right eye. I took a deep breath as he touched the lid, my lungs burned with every puff of air I took in. I managed to let a moan fall from my lips. He took an instrument from his bag, there was a light attached to the end of it. He shone it at the injured eye. He gently touched the surrounding area; I flinched, and Grams patted my hand in an effort to keep me calm.

Dr. Greene lifted the sheets that Grams used to cover me and looked at all the cuts and bruises that I had sustained on my legs and arms. "*Oh my*" was what he uttered when he looked further at my stomach, thighs and genitals. He announced that there was blood.

"She's still bleeding." The doctor said.

Grams shifted from one leg to the next. She remained at my side the entire time. Dr. Greene continued with the examination.

"Hmm" he let out another puzzled sound. "We need to get her to the hospital; she needs an internal examination, and a more thorough assessment than I could do for her here. Her fever is high, and we don't want her to go into shock. There is no time to be wasted, we need to take her there now. I'll drive."

Grams didn't wait for another word. She went into nurse mode again and wrapped me hurriedly but carefully – it was time to make a move. She motioned for my mother to help take me to the car, but it was Baby Boy who had to lift me once again. Momma sobbed, she could hardly look at me. Feebly I touched her hand when she got close and she whispered in an icy tone I had never heard from her before.

"I swear to God I'm going to find out who did this to you Bunny, Momma's gonna handle it, just you wait. I'm sorry Baby, Momma's so so sorry."

Her trembling hand held mine as Baby Boy carried me to Dr. Greene's waiting car.

We drove to the hospital in silence until I whispered to Grams.

"I just need my Daddy."

She touched my cheek.

When we arrived at the hospital, Dr. Greene asked us

to wait in the car while he rushed inside to get help. The hospital was only a few minutes from our house, so we got there in just a few minutes.

Dr. Greene disappeared inside the building but soon returned with an orderly and a wheelchair; a nurse was right behind them. I was helped out of the car by Grams and Momma, then I was gently led to the wheelchair by the nurse. I sat and was wheeled into a small room where another nurse quickly looked me over. Momma and Grams stayed close, and Baby Boy remained in the waiting area.

After the nurse checked my temperature and blood pressure, I was immediately taken into another room where a bed was ready and waiting. An IV was placed in my arm and the nurse proceeded to clean me up, I was given medication through the IV to help reduce the fever. I prayed for it to take effect as quickly as possible. Next I was given some pills which, the nurse warned, may be difficult to swallow; I took my time and tried hard to get them to pass down my throat. It hurt, but I did manage to get them down, and after a few minutes the turmoil that had been spinning inside me slowed to a manageable pace; the pain medication was working its magic. The rawness and burning subsided and I finally stopped shaking.

I could see Dr. Greene in a corner of the room as he spoke to the nurse who had been taking care of me. He came over after a few minutes and assured me that I was in good care, then left the room. Momma and Grams stood on the left and right sides of the cot that I laid on. I looked around for my friend Baby Boy, but he was nowhere to be seen; I wondered if he was still in the waiting area. Grams must have read my thoughts because she spoke to me and explained his whereabouts.

"He went on home, I told him there was no sense in him

waiting around any longer. Tell Grams who did this to you Sweetie, jus' tell me." She quickly changed the subject.

The tears spilled over onto her cheeks and flowed down her face; Momma watched silently with teary, bloodshot eyes; she patted my hand gently. I closed my eyes, and like Grams, I let the tears flow, but I remained silent. I wanted to sleep; I wanted to go to sleep and then wake up to find that this was all a terrible dream. I wanted to forget the whole episode. Grams squeezed my hand, giving me a signal that she would not push. I was happy that she chose not force me to relive the dreaded incident. Sleep was already taking me on a journey beyond the lights and movements in the room; I surrendered and let it take over. As I drifted off, I could still hear my Momma's cries.

CHAPTER SIX

The little thing moved and squirmed in the blanket; wailing like there was no-one else in the room. Ray looked at his newborn baby girl; perfect in every way, with ten fingers and ten toes and a head full of hair. She was the most beautiful creature his eyes had ever seen, and he had witnessed her taking her very first breath. Being there to see his little girl being delivered into the world was the greatest experience of his life. He wiped a tear from his eyes. He wanted to hold her forever.

Edna looked at her man holding his daughter; she knew from that moment that there was an unbreakable bond formed. She didn't mind one bit that Ray was so engrossed with the little thing; all she wanted to do at the moment was to get some sleep; she was exhausted from the experience.

"Ok Mr. Porter, we have to take her to the nursery now but as soon as she is cleaned up she will be ready to visit with you, and especially with Mom since she will be hungry."

Ray was amazed at how perfect his daughter was. She

had the biggest brown eyes he had ever seen, her black curly hair laid flat on her head. She was pink and gorgeous; he had contributed to the creation of this awesome little human. He was in love.

The nurse smiled at Ray as she took the baby from his arms and placed her into a bassinet, then wheeled it out of the room. He watched as the door closed. His heart was not big enough to hold the love he felt for his Princess; he couldn't wait to hold her again.

Ray turned his attention to Edna; she looked tired and happy all at the same time. The delivery was not difficult, but the labor was intense. Edna was a trooper though; she followed the directions of the doctors and nurses, and delivered his child – their baby. Ray walked to the bed where she lay; another nurse was busy making sure that the new Mom was doing ok and commended her for the great job she had done during the birthing process. Edna reached for Ray as he came closer. He kissed her on the forehead.

"She's beautiful, just like her Momma. We have a pretty little girl, Edna. Are you ok Baby?"

Edna shook her head. "I bet she looks just like her Daddy" she said.

Edna smiled.

"My mother should be here soon, Percy said he would let her know. She had to get a ride. That little girl is destined to be spoiled rotten."

They both laughed. They were parents of a brand new baby – life was good.

~~~~~~~~

Edna had gone into labor at Percy's house. It had happened while she, Ray, and Percy were sitting around a table playing cards. The mood was light and fun-filled as usual. Ray was winning, taking Percy's money before it had time to settle on the table.

"How the hell you gonna come into my house and try to take all my cash man?"

Percy pointed towards the door; shaking his hand and making the gesture as if to help his friend find the exit. Ray got up and pretended to move towards the door. Edna grabbed him and pulled him back.

"Nah Sugar, I'm leaving," Ray said jokingly in response to Edna's attempt to stop him.

He took his jacket and hat.

"Can a man win an honest game of Spades without being accused? Better yet, can't a man just take a whipping and stop whining like a little girl? I'm outta here."

Percy played along.

"Yea that's right, leave with your guilty conscience. You know you had hidden cards in your pockets. Who wears a long sleeved shirt, then rolls it up, then rolls it down again while playing such a serious game? Huh man? Tricks man, I knew it all along."

Percy could hardly contain his laughter, Ray joined in.

"Ray!" Edna yelled, "I think it's time Baby!"

Ray kept on walking and laughing, thinking that Edna was playing along with them too.

"Yea Edna, it's time for us to go, you ready Babe?"

"*NO RAY*" Edna shot back, almost screaming this time. "*THE BABY IS COMING NOW!*"

Ray stopped in his tracks and Percy got up quickly, almost knocking over the chair that he was sitting on. The two men got to Edna at the same time, both trying to help her up from her seating position. They scrambled about; Edna waited a few seconds for the chaos to be over, then instructed them on what to do. Ray was to get her bag, and Percy was to get his car keys and go wait outside in his car for them.

By this time Ray was drenched with sweat. He rummaged around the room looking for Edna's bag. It was in plain sight, but of course he missed it several times. He was nervous and excited. His mind was so scrambled that he almost ran through the door without Edna. She shook her head and sighed loudly. She panted and waddled as she made her way to Percy's car; finally her baby, their baby, was ready to make her appearance into the world.

The ride to the hospital was just as eventful with Ray yelling at Percy every time the car was driven over a bump or when they hit a pothole. He and Edna sat in the back seat, he fanned her, talked her through the contractions, and prayed that they would get to the hospital in time. It seemed like the minutes had turned into hours, making the short ride to the hospital longer than usual.

Edna tried the breathing techniques she had learned and practiced, but they seemed not be helping very much, the contractions were coming fast and furious. She just wanted the pain to stop. She grabbed Ray's hand with every one that she felt, and squeezed as hard as she could. She called out his name and that of her mother's too and hoped that she would not give birth in Percy's car.

The men tried to keep Edna as calm as possible during

the ride and when she felt like screaming, Ray encouraged her to focus on her breathing instead. She looked at him and did as he instructed, but like before it didn't do much to lessen the pain. Getting to the hospital and delivering this child was all that she really wanted to do?

After what seemed like forever, they finally arrived at the hospital. It was difficult to tell who was happiest of the three when they eventually pulled into the emergency driveway. One thing was for sure, they were all relieved that they arrived safely, and none was more so than Edna. Ray helped her to get out of the car and the medical personnel coming to her aide was a welcomed sight. She was wheeled into labor and delivery right away when a nurse was told that the contractions were less than a minute apart. She was happy that carrying this baby was almost at the end.

Labor went quickly. Everything happened at a fast pace, and at one point it all became a blur to Edna. The pain medicine barely had time to take effect before she heard the doctor telling her it was time to push. Ray talked softly to her, telling her that it would be alright. He counted with her, and he wiped her forehead with a damp cloth; he never left her side.

Percy paced back and forth nervously in the waiting area. Ida May arrived at the hospital and joined him. She too waited anxiously for the arrival of her grandchild. Percy could hardly wait for Ray to come out to make the announcement. It was just as if it was his baby being delivered.

When Raenelle Janine was born, Edna felt a great relief; finally the pain was gone, and she could see her baby. The nurse rested the wrinkled little thing on Edna's chest and she barely had time to look at her new daughter before Ray took the blanketed child and started cooing, talking to her like she understood his words. Now she was out of the room and they were alone. They cried happy tears of joy.

CHAPTER SEVEN

Pearl looked at her image in the mirror; it was hard to believe that she was finally getting married. She was already 32, way past the expected age to be someone's wife, yet alone a mother. At this point in her life, she should already have at least 2 children.

'Oh well, better late than never' she thought to herself.

It took a lot of work to get here though; getting Jimmy Truitt to even look at her was a task. There was a long line of women waiting and hoping, and her turn seemed to take forever. She knew he was a womanizer, a drunk of sorts, and an arrogant fool, but it was the challenge of being able to change him, and having his children that attracted her to him. Her mother's constant nagging about her becoming an old hag was enough to drive Pearl to do whatever it took to get Jimmy or some other eligible man to give her the time of day. To help with her quest, Pearl hung around the town's socialites, sticking her nose into the businesses of people who couldn't care less about her. She used her mother's career as a legal secretary for a well-known attorney as her claim to have a position among them.

Her mother got all the news and gossip from her boss' clientele, and passed them on to Pearl. Of course she concocted stories and blew things out of proportion to make them more dramatic. Although Pearl did not call names, she just gave good hints as to what was going on with almost every family around town. She gave enough information to peak her friends' interest, but as little as possible so as not to disclose any detail that could get her mother in trouble. There was no telling if someone would go back to the attorney and tell him that information had been leaked *from his office.*

Almost every case that was handled at the law office, was discussed by Pearl and her mother over dinner, so when in the company of others, Pearl spoke as if she knew all about the law. The women in certain circles loved this type of chatter, and it helped to keep her spot among the socialites who were nosey gossipers. It was at one of these chatty gossiping social events where she first met Jimmy Truitt.

He had a woman hanging from his arm, she looked at least 10 years his senior, but it was obvious that there was more going on between them than just casual acquaintances. Jimmy always had a female companion at his side, it was his thing, what he was known for. Although he referred to these women as just friends, there was no secret that Jimmy was a man who bedded many of them; he spread his love all over town.

His companion that night made sure that her body touched his – she leaned into him when she spoke – certain indication that she had been captured by his spell. The woman made circles on his back with her perfectly manicured red nails, batting her eyes and sipping her drink, making all her movements look seductive.

Pearl watched the pair for the entire night. She placed herself in a position to be close enough to get a good view. When the 'hanger-on' left for the ladies room, another woman *quickly* stepped into her spot, vying for a chance to get with Jimmy, he thrived on the attention.

Pearl was well aware that she was not the only one with eyes on him, so all that groping and pushing up did not bother her too much. Jimmy was not really a handsome man, she concluded, but he had a certain charismatic way and a lovely charm that created a presence about him. He like to show off his athletic body; wearing shirts that sometimes looked a size too small. She attributed his built to his training from his military days.

Pearl knew a bit about Jimmy's personal life. She had heard that he was a driven young man, served his country in the army. When he returned to Jessup he was placed in charge of the Criminal Investigative Division of the local police department. This was a great accomplishment for a young man; he instantly became an eligible bachelor, a title he took without a fuss; an authoritative position in the law gave him top choice of women. Pearl's mother thought he was someone that her daughter should introduce herself to; it was time for her to find to a husband, and Jimmy Truitt was the right man.

The *Police Benevolent Association* dinner wore on for a through the night, Pearl was really bored, she had been there since 6:30pm that evening. The loud music and chatter were starting to get irritating. She was a guest at the event because she was hoping for an opportunity to see Jimmy; she would take advantage of the chance to meet him if it presented itself.

She sat at a table with her mother and Mr. Pennington,

her mother's boss. Her friend Harriet had left earlier because she fell ill during the *Medal of Honor* presentation. Her departure meant that Pearl would either have to sit and listen to her mother criticize other people or chatter about cases with Mr. Pennington, or walk around for a bit and try to find another of her 'friends' that she could converse with until she found Jimmy or was ready to leave. She decided on the latter. She excused herself from the table on the guise that she had to use the facilities in the ladies room but knew full well that she just really wanted to walk around. There was no telling who she would run into that way.

The dinner and awards ceremony was held at the Grand Hotel downtown Jessup; the venue was very nicely decorated, valet parking, hat and coat check, white gloved servers, and assigned tables were all a part of the set up.

Pearl eventually found the bathroom, the attendant opened the door and she stepped into the warmly lit; small baskets of products – lotions, facial tissue packets, etc., lined the counter; there was a jar for tips beside a glass bowl with mints. Pearl stepped closer so that she could take a good look at herself in the mirror; her hair was still in place, a bun at the crown of her head with strands of her golden hair hanging haphazardly about her face; it suited her. She took her face powder compact from her bag and patted her face with the puff. She reapplied crimson lipstick to her lips – she wished that they were a bit more pouty, but oh well, she had to love herself as she was, nothing could be done about that right now. She fixed the strap of her black floor length gown and then walked out of the room. She tipped the attendant $2.00 as she exited.

As soon as she turned the corner to head to the bar, it happened -she bumped into *him* – Jimmy Truitt!! And for a moment, they stood, eye to eye. Her heart rate accelerated.

"I'm sorry" Pearl stuttered nervously.

"No, no, it's my fault. I should have paid attention."

Jimmy held her by the waist to help steady her; she had stumbled a bit.

"Here, let me get that" He picked up her purse which dropped when their bodies collided and handed it to her. None of its contents spilled out much to her relief.

After ensuring that the lady was ok and composed, and when he was sure that she was ready Jimmy gestured to the bar. He asked Pearl to allow him to buy her a drink to make up for the collision he caused. She allowed him to lead her there. When the bartender came over to take their order, Jimmy asked for seltzer and a lemon wedge for Pearl and a straight scotch for himself. They did formal introductions, shook hands casually and then turned their attentions to their respective drinks.

Pearl was a bit nervous and intimidated but she held herself together; after all she could not have asked for a better thing to happen to her; the meeting happened as it was orchestrated by God. She kept smiling, and mimicked the eye batting and lean in laughter she had seen other women do; this was what she hoped would be the thing to keep his interest.   They stood as the bar for a long period of time, chatting and laughing as they got to know each other. The remainder of the evening was spent this way.

Fortunately for Pear, the woman who was with him earlier at this event, was nowhere in sight; Pearl was pleased; she could have him all to herself, at least for now. As she relaxed, she began to feel more comfortable with him just sitting there and talking. He looked straight into her eyes when he spoke to her, something that made her feel tingly and nervous at the same time. His actions could have been due to the alcohol but she did not care. At the end of the evening, she gave Jimmy her contact information and assured him that she enjoyed his company; he kissed her on the cheek after he had walked her back to her table. The night, for her, was a success.

After their chance encounter that night, Jimmy made it his business to visit Pearl at her home; they would meet for coffee or at the park and any other place they had the opportunity to, he even visited her at her workplace once or twice per week. After several dinner dates and outings with friends, they officially became a couple. Pearl rubbed shoulders with wives of mayors, congressmen, businessmen, and other high ranking officials. This was the kind of life she loved – she had dreamed of this all of her life. Jimmy was the right man for her – she just knew it, and theirs' was a true budding romance *in her eyes*. Through it all Jimmy remained sweet and attentive, she felt good to be by his side. *Pearl* had finally *arrived*.

Ten months later they decided to tie the knot; they would be joined in matrimony. No-one, except Pearl and Jimmy, knew why they were in such a rush to tie the knot. The real reason would be kept secret until 2 months after the wedding. Pearl dared not tell her mother that she was pregnant prior to the nuptials; it would bring embarrassment to the woman who lived by how others in society viewed her. An unwed pregnant daughter was not in Gladys's plan; that would take her to an early grave for sure.

Pearl had long decided that an abortion was out of the question, it was not even an option, especially at her age. This pregnancy may be her only chance to have a child. Besides, there was no way she could remain in the circle she fought so hard to get into, if she had a *bastard* child. When she gave Jimmy the news, he was less than thrilled but after some heated discussions, he agreed that marriage was the only option; he would take care of his responsibilities. Furthermore, he admitted to Pearl that it was timed that he got married and settled; it would look good for his career as well.

CHAPTER EIGHT

Lester grimaced as the other player's helmet crashed into his stomach; being the star quarterback on the school's football team had its perks, but getting sacked was not one of them. His body would ache at the end of games or practices, so much so that at times he would sit in the tub with warm water and bath salts to help sooth his aching muscles. Tonight his concentration was off; he was tired and unfocused. He had hardly slept the night before because he was haunted by the image of the girl he and Eugene had left in the woods.

'The girl' he thought to himself as if he didn't know who she was; he'd known her since she was a little girl. This made him feel heavy with guilt. He tried to remember the play that he was supposed to make but his game was off, his usual quick moves were absent today, and his coach and team-mates noticed. He had just suffered his third sack in the quarter; something that never happened before. Frank, one of the other players, helped him up. He shook his head in an effort to regain his focus and composure; he needed to get his mind back on the game. A whistle blew to signal the end of play– much to his relief. Lester and the other players ran off the field towards the bench where the

rest of the team sat and the coach waited. Coach Dickens rushed over to him and began barking his displeasure at Lester's performance.

"You are the damned backbone of this team boy, so you'd better get your ass in game mode 'fore we lose this game. Our record is at stake here, you hear me son? Now get your eyes moving, your mind thinking of nothing but the game, and you focus! You know the plays, now come on!"

Lester nodded to the coach; he was right, his performance sucked. He tried his best to think about what he needed to do to lead his team to victory. The words of Coach Dickens rang in his ears.

'Come on Lester, you can do this! Focus!' He said to himself.

After the coach walked away, Lester quickly searched the sea of faces in the bleachers for his brother. He was not in his usual spot; normally Eugene was front and center at his brother's games. Lester spun around and scoured the area once more, Eugene was nowhere in sight.

'Maybe he went to the concession stand' he thought. This was more to convince himself that there was nothing wrong, and that he shouldn't worry. The thing they did was still a secret between them.

If his brother was in the crowd watching the game, it meant that all was well; that no one had found out. Lester had told Eugene that they should have dragged the body in a more bushy area of the woods, but Eugene insisted that it was better to leave her where they did; in the open for easier access to wild animals.

"Wild animals are always out in them here woods,"

Eugene had said. "One will come along and eat her, we should just leave that slut be; let a bear or some other kind of wild creature get their taste too."

They had both laughed at that statement; at the time it was funny, but now it only echoed in Lester's mind; it was beginning to torment him. He knew that those swigs of whiskey would've clouded his judgment and he would do things against his judgment, but he wanted to please his brother – as usual.

The whistle blew again; this time signaling that the next quarter was about to begin. Lester put on his helmet and placed his mouth guard back in. He didn't hear anything that was said, or what strategy they decided on to beat the other team, he was too busy trying to locate his brother in the stands. He shook his head as the coach slapped him on his back and shouted encouraging words at him. Lester turned and gave the coach a thumbs-up, but he also took one last scan of the area where Eugene usually sat; he spotted his brother. He breathed a sigh of relief.

Confirmation that Eugene was in the crowd must have given Lester a boost of confidence, because for the rest of the game he played like the star he was, calling plays, finding his teammates, and throwing perfect touchdown passes. The final score was Black Hawks 21, Bears 17; they won by sheer luck; thank God for the sign. When they got to the locker room, Lester got a good scolding from Coach Dickens.

"Boy, I don't know what's going on with you, but you'd better get it together 'fore next week's game. The team is dependin' on you Son. Make your Papa proud boy, bring home that trophy. Stay focused and get back to game mode. I need that fire to return Son! You hear me? We need this!"

The coach turned his attention to the rest of the team,

most of whom were undressing and getting ready to hit the showers.

"Now listen up here fellas, next week we have one game, and winning that game will take us into the semis. I don't have to tell you how important winning the State Championship title is. I expect all of you to show up to every practice; no hanky panky nonsense either, and none of you get into any trouble. Sherriff Whitfield will be on the lookout, and he will report back to me. No drinking, no unruly behavior at the local hangouts, none of that. I hope you all are paying attention to my every word. Stay out of trouble! Now go on and get y'all selves cleaned up, and head on home. We'll celebrate once the State Championship is won!" The team let out a bird call in unison, then filed into the shower room.

Lester swallowed hard, he flashed back to the girl they left to die; if anyone found out, it would be hell to pay, and in more than one way. He stood silently let the water wash away all the dirt and grime from his body; he wanted the water to take away the memories from *last night* as well.

Normally he would be chatting up a storm with the other boys or lollygagging around after showers, but today he just needed to hurry up and get out. He wanted to meet Eugene to suggest that they return to the woods and find the body, then bury it. He wasn't sure if his brother would want to go, but he would insist that they should, just to be sure that no animal would drag the girl out in the open, or so that no one would come across her by chance. Lester quickly got dressed and grabbed his bag from his locker, then ran through the halls on his way out to the bleachers where Eugene always waited for him. He had to find him and go back to the place they were last night.

When he got to the main corridor that led to the field,

Lester stopped; he spotted his brother, but he also saw Sherriff Whitfield in full uniform talking to him. Lester's heart pounded in his chest. Instinct told him to turn around, but his feet refused to move. Beads of sweat began to form around his forehead; his body felt weak. Eugene looked up and noticed him; he waved for him to join them. '*Why would he do that?* Lester asked himself. Eugene was not thinking straight, he was certain. With all the will-power he could muster, Lester walked toward Sheriff Whitfield and his brother. Eugene was not stupid enough to let anything out, he couldn't be; he was sure of that.

His brother was tough, and could not be broken; he had seen that many times when their father scolded him or took the strap to him for some trouble he had gotten into. Eugene would never tell anyone they had raped and killed a girl, and Miss Edna's girl at that. She was nothing but trash anyway; at least that's what Eugene had said when they were torturing her. Trash – that made him forget for an instant that she was human; he could sure use a swig of whiskey at this moment.

As soon as Lester got close enough to hear, Sherriff Whitfield stated to speak.

"Lemme tell you boy, you were on fire out there."

Sheriff Whitfield laughed and everything jiggled; he was a very large man about 6'5" and over 200 pounds. Any criminal could outrun him, but his size and height put fear into the most callous of law breakers. The Sherriff continued to give praises to Lester.

"I tell you boy, the way you threw them balls Son, they was guaranteed to be touchdowns, hahaha. Other people were panicking, thinkin' that y'all was about to lose that game, but not me Son. I had confidence the whole time."

Every body part of the Sherriff's shook once more. He slapped Lester on the back.

"Your Daddy sure did pass on them skills to ya; make sure to keep that up Son."

The same thunderous laughter echoed once again. Lester gave a half smile, hoping not to give his real feelings of fear away.

"Yes sir, thank you sir."

He looked over at Eugene. His brother looked calm and relaxed; he chewed on the twig he had in his mouth; he always had a piece there. There was no sign displayed that Eugene was worried about what they did last night; no uneasy movements, no nervous twitches, nothing at all showed on the outside.

"Well boys you go on now, go do y'all boys' things."

Sherriff Whitfield walked towards the locker room. Lester's shoulders relaxed and he let out a deep sigh. Then it happened.

"Oh, by the way boys" the Sherriff turned around and walked towards them, "lemme ask ya'll a question, I don't want to take up too much more of y'all's time so I'll be quick".

The Sherriff adjusted his suspenders, then continued.

"There's been a little chatter in town 'bout somethin' in them there woods, you know Pleasant Creek Park. Dr. Greene came into the office to report an incident; I can't really give too much details, y'all understand. Now boys, Jessup is a good town here in Georgia, we are a peaceful and lovin' community and we don't like trouble, so if you boys know anything, you can tell me. If you heard any talk or saw anything strange about, then this is a good time to say somethin'."

Sherriff Whitfield took two steps to the short corridor wall and spat over it; then wiped the brown slime that dripped from his lips. It's a good thing that there was grass and gravel on the other side. The awful smelling liquid that lingered on the Sheriff's shirt made Lester feel like throwing up. The sleeve was already stained with the awful color of snuff. Lester looked over at his brother, he still stood stoic. Still maintaining his composure. Lester's heart began to race once more. The loud thud echoed in his ear, drowning out any thoughts that may have entered into his brain.

Eugene spoke, "no sir, Sherriff sir, we ain't hear nothing about nothing. What happened Sherriff and what girl?" he asked innocently.

Lester wanted to run, he wished he could make a mad dash and go as far as his feet could take him. He tried to stay calm, but could feel his body starting to betray him; he shifted from one leg to the next and averted his eyes to his hands.

"Ah you boys don't concern yourselves, if ya'll don't know 'bout the troubles found in the woods, then no problem. Just keep an ear out for anything you hear that's not custom and report it to my office."

Sherriff Whitfield spat once more, nodded to the boys, and then walked away. As soon as he was out of earshot, Eugene grabbed Lester and pushed him toward the parking lot to the spot where his pickup truck was waiting.

Eugene spoke with clenched teeth to his younger brother.

"You stupid fool, you could've given away everything.

I'm pretty darned sure if that fat idiot had asked you, you'd have told him everything. You were shaking and lookin' all frightened. What is your problem? Are you a man or a little punk bitch?"

Lester said nothing. They had reached the parking area and were standing near Eugene's red pickup truck. It was a gift from their father presented to him on his 16th birthday. It was a bit beaten, but it was reliable; it took them everywhere they wanted to go, and it held many secrets.

Lester threw his football gear unto the bed of the truck and walked around to the passenger side. He got into the vehicle without saying a word to his brother, he looked straight ahead. Eugene started the engine and the pickup jumped forward, sputtered, then finally the engine revved, and the truck moved forward. Eugene turned unto the dirt road that would lead them out of the school compound and onto the main road in the direction of their house.

"Listen here Eugene I think we need to go back to the woods and make sure that that piece of nothing girl was torn to shreds. It was just last night so if the animals did not tear her apart then we'll find the body and bury it."

Lester sat stoned faced; he was serious about his plan. He tried to sound tough, but deep down inside he was afraid, and that old guilt was starting to creep in stronger than before. It was Miss Edna's girl that they had done what they did to, he minded himself once more. Miss Edna, the woman they knew for most of their lives, the woman who practically raised them. He waited for Eugene to respond to what he had suggested.

"Are you fucking crazy?" His brother spat angrily at him. "Didn't you hear Whitfield? He asked about something happening in the woods; he knows something. I ain't going back there, I won't take a chance and get caught. Knowing that fat bastard, he's probably waiting for us to step foot at the place of crime. He knows something Lester. No way man, we're ain't going back. Let her rot! It's a stupid idea you have there boy!"

Eugene kept on driving, he took glances at his brother and waited for him to say something. Lester just stared straight ahead. The guilt had completed its creeping and was now settled.

~~~~~~~~

Eugene stepped on the brakes suddenly, the jolt of the pickup truck flung Lester forward, and he crashed into the dashboard almost banging his head on the windshield. Eugene reached over, grabbed him and shouted.

"Listen here asshole, we are not going back there! Think Lester, com' on man, think! They know something happened, what excuse could we use if we got caught in that area, huh? Why the hell do you care now about the girl?"

Lester looked at his brother; he wanted to tell him to go to hell, but he knew better. Eugene could make him do *anything*; he had that type of control over him. After all, his big brother was the reason he was still here on earth today, he felt like he owed him his life.

~~~~~~~~

It was a quiet summer day, the temperature was the highest they had had in years, 98 degrees and it was only 10:00am.

"You boys be careful now, there is no running in the kitchen. It's too hot to get so worked up and this room is no place for busy boys to play."

Edna was busy getting things organized to make lunch, and the boys were driving her crazy – running around the house from room to room, yelling and screaming.

She repeated this warning several times but the boys continued to run around, chasing after their shadows and laughing as they did. When they almost knocked a tray of just baked cookies from her hands, Edna stopped them in their tracks. She managed to put the tray on the counter without spilling the contents, then grabbed each boy by the arm. She knelt to their level.

"I think it's best if you both go into the yard for a minute."

"It's hot outside Miss Edna, we don't want to."

Eugene, the older of the two and the defiant one, pouted his lips.

"I'm almost done frying the chicken, hot oil is very dangerous, and the way you two are running in here, one of you is bound to get burned. You're both lucky that the tray of cookies I was holding didn't drop on one of you."

Edna opened the door and let them out.

"Five or so minutes is all I need, and don't you go out those back gates either."

The boys went under the elm tree that was in the middle of the backyard. The shade was nice but with no breeze blowing, it was really sticky and hot. For a few minutes they drew circles in the dirt with twigs that had fallen to the ground; they made different shapes and tried to guess what each other had drawn. It was fun for a minute but soon they were bored of that.

"Let's go put our toes in the pond Lester."

The pond was about 20 feet wide, and about 12 feet at its deepest point. According to what Edna said, it was dug out by Confederate soldiers in 1863 during the Civil War. She was not sure what they used it for back then but assumed that the soldiers had a good reason for it.

Eugene, 12 years old at the time, looked at his brother.

"Miss Edna says we're not supposed to go past the back gate."

Lester shook his head as he spoke.

"Aw come on, we'll only put our toes in."

Eugene checked to make sure that Edna was not watching.

"Besides, Miss Edna is not our Momma, she can't tell us what to do."

Lester, not wanting to appear scared, nodded his agreement, but his heart raced. They checked to make sure that neither Miss Edna nor anyone else was looking. They confirmed that their mother was asleep in her room and Miss Edna appeared to be still busy in the kitchen. The boys then lifted the latch of the gate and made their way to the pond. The water was still, Eugene was first to put his right foot in.

"See, the water is not even cold. It feels good Lester, try."

Reluctantly, Lester put his foot in the water also, it did feel good. He smiled at his brother. He put both feet and stepped further in; it was great! He wanted to go further, one more step. It was a hot day, he wanted to feel the water all over his body. They never swam in the pond without a grown-up present, but he wanted to show his brother that he was brave.

Just one dip, and then he would run out quickly. The next thing Lester remembered was Eugene calling his name and pressing on his chest telling him to breathe. He was lying, totally drenched, on the bank of the lake. He coughed and water came from his nose and mouth.

"We need to get Miss Edna" Lester whispered.

Eugene convinced him that it was not the right thing to do. He said that they would be in more trouble because they were not supposed to be outside of the gate. Lester sat up and took some more breaths. He felt better after a while. Eugene snuck back home and got him some dry clothes to change into, he hid the wet ones under some shrubs behind the barn. No one ever found out; it was a secret they kept to this day.

Now here they were, Eugene calling the shots as usual.

"Alright, we'll think of something else."

Lester rubbed his shoulder; he had slammed it pretty hard.

"Good, now you're making sense. Let's go home, I'm sure supper's ready."

Eugene playfully slapped Lester on the head, then drove on.

CHAPTER NINE

After the birth of her first son, Eugene, Pearl went into a feeling of emptiness and sadness that she'd never experienced before. He physician diagnosed her and concluded that she was suffering from post-partum depression. It was a terrible thing, she thought, for a new mother not to want to hold her baby boy – not even when he cried. She would feed him while he was propped up on pillows, in the chair, or on the bed. She never held him in her lap nor nestle him to her breast. There was no bonding at all; the joy she thought she would feel from having a child never came.

Pearl's mother, Gladys, tried desperately to get her to be more doting, and tried desperately to show her how she should mother the boy, she encouraged her; tried to coerce her and would put the baby close to Pearl when he cried. Pearl would sometimes fall asleep only to wake up and find the child lying next to her, she would stare at him as he squirmed or cooed; she only wanted to go to another room; away from him. Nothing anyone could do helped the situation.

The father was not really a better parent as far as giving

the child the attention he deserved as a newborn. At nights when Jimmy would come home from work, he would barely look at Eugene. There were times when he would just pick him up if he was in the room, hold him outward at arms' length, and say something about the boy growing too fat, taking too long to talk, or he that he needed to be changed. After that Jimmy would retire to his office or sit in front of the television for the remainder of the night. That was the extent of the interaction with his first son.

Pearl ultimately resolved that motherhood was not for her, it was not what she thought it would be, the demands were just too much. A baby required a lot of attention, and she didn't want her entire day filled up with taking care of a child. She wanted her old life back. She missed being able to socialize, plan events, and meet with the other women in her circle. In addition to that, Jimmy had recently started coming home later and later at nights; barely speaking, just eating dinner, then watching television before going straight to sleep. He explained that the demands of his job kept him at the office late. This was his excuse whenever Pearl began to complain about not spending time with her and the baby.

Jimmy's lack of interest in his family drove Pearl into an even deeper depression. It got so bad at one point that she decided she needed someone to help care for the child in order to maintain her sanity. She made the decision to stay with her mother during the week and then return to her him on weekends. Being alone all day with a child she could not shower with maternal attention and the disrespect from her husband was just too much to bear. Jimmy was all too happy to go along with the arrangements; he happily dropped them off and picked them up as needed.

Two years and two months after Eugene's birth, Pearl

discovered that she was pregnant again. She wanted to get rid of it, she did not want any more children; the first was enough.

She had begun her socializing again, gotten back into her circles, and was feeling like her old self once more. She knew that she did not want to carry another child for nine months again; it would surely hinder her from life as it was. The first time with the excitement of being pregnant had surely fizzled after the birth, and besides, the boy, at his age, was not as independent as he should be. He finally stated to walk unassisted a moth shy of his second birthday, but he still asked to be picked up or would crawl instead. It would be too much now: taking care of Eugene, doing her events, and caring for another baby. She would surely go mad.

Young Eugene spent most days with Gladys. His grandmother loved to have him around. It was obvious that since Pearl returned to her socializing she was happier, even Jimmy's late night working was not as bothersome to her as it was before. She had other things to take her mind off of her troubled family matters.

Pearl was adamant about the untimeliness of her second pregnancy!

She discussed the issue with her mother; she tried hard to convince Gladys that it would serve no purpose to have another baby. Of course in her mother's eyes, not going through the pregnancy was of the question and would have nothing to do with an abortion. He pointed out that the procedure was illegal, that the risks were too great, and most importantly, she saw this baby as another opportunity to help Pearl keep Jimmy as her husband. Everyone was aware of his extramarital affairs.

"One child is not a guarantee that a husband would

stay around." Gladys said to her daughter. She continued,

"You should tell your husband about this, he has a right to know."

That was her mother's final input; there was to be no further discussions. Pearl gave Jimmy the news one evening over dinner and to her surprise he was elated; she was shocked. The sudden change took her for a loop. He hardly spent time with Eugene; barely knew much about his daily activities and accomplishments; chances are it would be the same with the second child. Pearl pretended to be just as happy as her husband, she played along, pushing the thought of an abortion as the back of her mind for now.

Jimmy turned out to be genuinely happy and finally started to things a good husband would for his wife. He accompanied her to doctor's appointments, bought her the foods she liked, and even rubbed her feet without her having to ask. Pearl began to enjoy being pregnant; she finally started to feel that this time would be different – pleasant – to say the least. Her previous thoughts of an abortion eventually dissipated.

The hands on attention she received from her husband made Pearl feel special; so much so that Eugene seemed less of a burden now. The good thing about this was that he would have a sibling to play with, giving Pearl a bit more freedom when she was alone at home with them. Her life was finally getting better; more like what she envisioned prior to her marriage. A happy home, and a happy family! Pearl even put her social life on hold, making herself less available to her friends. She turned her attention and focus on plans for the arrival of the new baby. She relaxed and enjoyed it all.

The second child arrived; it was another boy. Jimmy

named him Lester in honor of his grandfather; his full name being *Lester George Truitt*. He was different from his older brother, he looked just like Jimmy. Pearl loved her new born baby more than the first; she secretly wished that he was the only child she had had. Jimmy was happy too, he spent more time with his younger son than he did with the older. He wanted to make things different; at least that's what he explained.

Eugene took to his baby brother instantly; he showered him with love, always wanting to kiss him and to share his toys. He was very protective of Lester never letting him out of his sight for more than a minute. The first two years with the new baby were wonderful as far as family unity; Pearl couldn't ask for any better. Soon after though, the rumors started.

At first Pearl just brushed it off as lies, as the doings of some vindictive person who wanted to destroy her happiness. The first time she heard the whispers she had gone out with her children. She decided to take them with her to the neighborhood grocery store. Normally she would it was the housekeeper's chore to go shopping for foodstuff, but she decided to do it herself for a change. Besides, the outing would be good for the baby.

She held Eugene's hand while pushing Lester in the fancy baby carriage that her mother had bought. It was a natural colored wicker body carriage, with a velour hood that could be adjusted to shield the sun. It had chrome frame, and sturdy oversized white tires. It was the best of the best. Gladys had went all out for her second grandson.

Several ladies from her mother's social circle were also at the market. They cooed and awed at the boys, and paid extra special attention to Lester. They particularly liked his chubby cheeks; they were magnets. Eugene stood close to the carriage, keeping an eye on his baby brother.

Pearl noticed a group of four mulatto women standing a few yards away. One was very pregnant, she looked like she could have the child at any given moment.

"Do you know her?"

One of the women who was playing with Lester asked casually.

"How would I know her?"

Pearl was taken aback by the question. How would she possibly know that woman?

"Hmmm" was the woman's response.

"Am I supposed to know her?"

No one answered her. They all looked every which way except at Pearl. The woman who had asked the question kissed the boys, while the other two women whispered; then they all said their goodbyes and walked away.

Pearl kept her eyes on the mulatto women, especially the one who was pregnant; the woman returned her stare. Pearl could not deny that she was very beautiful. Her round freckled face displayed two deep dimples when she smiled; Pearl found herself mesmerized by the woman's radiance. She wore a long white dress that hugged every part of her body. She and the other women looked over at Pearl soon they began to whisper. Pearl felt uneasy and left the market without making a purchase.

When she returned home she called her mother and told her about the incident. If Gladys knew anything or heard any rumors she would certainly tell her daughter about it. Her mother suggested that she ignore what she saw and concentrate on keeping her children and husband happy. She assured her that there was nothing for her to tell. Pearl could tell when her mother was hiding information from her but she decided not to press the issue. At the back of her mind she kept the image of the pregnant woman.

CHAPTER TEN

After Raenelle's birth, Ray worked more hours at the factory. It was a tough decision but one he had to make in order make ends meet. Supporting his family was the only thing that mattered to him although he felt he missed valuable time with his baby girl. She was growing nicely, Edna was an excellent mommy to their daughter and Ray felt blessed and proud to have them both in his life.

They had planned to move in together as a family, but Edna's mother protested; her devout faith ruled her house. She proclaimed that it was bad enough that her daughter had a baby out of wedlock, she had gotten over that when she saw her beautiful granddaughter, but she was not about to have Edna become the talk of Jessup by shacking up, still unmarried. She even point out that although they had talks that about living together, neither of the two had ever mentioned marriage.

Ida May put her foot down and demanded that Edna and the baby remain at her home and she easily won the battle. Ray was not sure that he could maintain his family on his own with the wages he made at the factory anyway therefore he did not argue with Edna's mother. He didn't want to have them live from pay check to pay check. It was good that Ida May was adamant about Edna not following in her footsteps; no living together and then end up waiting and waiting to get married. She wanted to make certain that her daughter maintained a respectable image.

~~~~~~~~

Ida May had defied many odds during her time in Jessup. She was born to parents who were still indentured, working as field hands for the owners of the main plantation in their small town. They worked from sun up until sun down and for minimal pay. Sometimes her mother would return home with bleeding hands, but that did not stop her from preparing her family's meals. She never let the pain of any kind stop her from her duties as a wife and mother. She declared that she was put on the earth to do exactly what she was doing and that complaining would change none of it!

Ida May vowed from early in her life that she would not be a field worker. Just like her mother, she had certain things imbedded in her mind about how she viewed life and she was sure that she would do better. As soon as she was able, she found a job as a dishwasher in the kitchen of the local hospital. She put all of her energy into being the best at her tasks; her work ethics did not go unnoticed and eventually she worked her way up to supervisor. However, her career of choice was to become a registered nurse and eventually become a charge nurse.

With her determination to succeed she would soon become a nurse's aide. This happened after finally being accepted into and attending classes offered by the only nursing school in Jessup. She had tried several times to get into the school, going to the head of the institution each time she was rejected. It was her right to get a valid explanation as to why she was not accepted. Ida May was sure that she had passed the entrance examination each time that she had taken it. Each time she spoke to the admissions director she was given some made up story or another. All the white students were filling the classes, and only one or two Blacks were accepted just so fill a quota. The reason for her rejection was as clear as day!

Ida May remained relentless, she went back to take the test 7 times, finally she received the good news about her acceptance; she had received the highest scores as she was sure she had done on past exams. This time they had run out of excuses to reject her. She immediately secured a position at the same hospital where she had given her service for so long; it felt good to finally be something other than a worker in the kitchen; she could give great care directly to patients.

That was not the end for Ida, she continue her studies to become a registered nurse – the ultimate desire of her heart. There was nothing that could stop her that is until she met a man named Harold and became pregnant.

The baby came and slowed down Ida's fast past to fulfil her career plans.

She and Harold met at the hospital where she worked; he had come to visit a sick uncle who had a terminal illness. His visits lasted an extended period of time until his uncle eventually passed away. Ida comforted him, offered her support in his time of grieve, and became his source of strength. The two became close and developed strong feelings for one another.

Harold was sweet, even after the birth of their baby. He promised her the world and vowed to marry her, but whenever she asked him how soon they would exchange vows he always had a reason to hold off - he had some matters to attend to in New York - was his most favored. He told her that he would be in a better position to be a husband and father when the business was completed he would return for her and their daughter. That's story is what he stuck to and Ida May believed him. There was no way he would lie to her after all h was her man!

Prior to his departure to New York, he asked her to borrow some money – the amount he needed was what she had in her savings account. She had scrimped and put aside all she could so that she could finish her nursing education. Because she was in love and the man was the father of her child, Ida gave him the money. Harold in turn told her that his trip would only be for a few weeks and promised that after his business was concluded Ida May would be able continue her schooling in New York when she joined him there.

She believed every word he said and when he had been gone for a week packed her things and anxiously waited for her love to return. She excitedly looked forward to a new life in New York, it would be good to get away from Jessup and it would be good for Edna to grow up in a different part of the country.

A few weeks turned into months, then months into years. Ida May never heard from Harold again.

~~~~~~~~

The more time that went by, the more Ray thought about joining the military. Percy was ready to pack his bags and get out of Jessup at a moment's notice. The factory work was tedious and unfulfilling. Ray did his best to be an actively involved father, and juggling daddy duties when he could and the long hours at work were very demanding; providing for a baby was proving to be no joke.

For a little person, his daughter needed so much.

Ida May did her best to help them and, as any good mother and grandmother would, contributed to the wellbeing of her daughter and granddaughter. Even though Ida did these things for Edna and the baby Ray felt it was his duty to take care of his family. He wanted more from life than working at a dead-end job; he wanted to be more than *this life* for himself, and even more so for his baby girl. He felt it was his duty to ensure that she her future was secure enough to not have to worry about getting what she wanted, needed and deserved. However, until then, he had to be the one to create a foundation on which she could build. That was his responsibility, not anyone else's!

Ray finally made his decision. He accepted that that joining the military, specifically the Marines, would be his best chance to make a positive change for himself and the family he would have to leave behind. It would not be an easy thing especially since his daughter was about to celebrate her first birthday. It had to be now or never, recruitment was done – there was no turning back.

His ultimate plan was to serve his to serve his country for two tours of duty and then he would come back a better man for his family, being there when she was older would still allow him to be the father he knew he could be. Edna would understand his need to make this move, she had to.

They had already passed the written and physical exams - the first steps for him and his friend Percy. Boot camp and training were next; then there could be no turning back. He was ready and it had to be done. A better life lay ahead for all of them.

The men left the military facility where the tests were conducted then Percy dropped his friend off at Edna's house. Ray could hear Raenelle's laughter coming from inside, they were playing hide and seek; Edna counted down 10 to 1, giving Rae time to hide.

Jessup was humid that summer, rain would be a welcomed change in the weather; the place was dry, not a bit off breeze could be felt. Ray was a big man, physically but he suddenly felt small walking up the steps to the home where his woman and daughter lived. He was about to tell them both that he would be absent from their lives for months at a time for the next 4 or so years. It would be a bitter sweet moment; he was not looking forward to breaking the news.

"Daddy, Daddy."

Raenelle ran to her father as soon as he walked through the door. He picked her up and spun her around; she squealed with delight. Edna stood watching the pair; there was no denying that theirs' was an unbreakable bond.

"I love you Princess."

Ray nuzzled his daughter's neck with the tip of his nose. She giggled even more. Listening to her laughter, and having the proud feeling of being the father of this little girl, made Ray tear up; he would miss his baby.

CHAPTER ELEVEN

Baby Boy peered through the window, waiting for the moment when Percy's yellow Thunderbird would drive up the street. That would be confirmation that Miss Edna was returning from the hospital. He was worried about his friend.

That night it was Baby Boy who had found Percy and told him what had happened; he went on a mission to find him right after he left the hospital. He knew that Percy would be at his bar and so he delivered the news to him there. As soon as he heard the first words about his god-daughter, Percy jumped into his car and raced to be at his her side. He had to be there for her.

Baby Boy had not seen or heard anything since the night before and he was anxious to know how his best friend was doing. He moved the curtain to the far corner of the window; he didn't want anything to block his view. He glanced over at his mother who sat on her favorite chair, rocking back and forth with her Bible clenched in her hands. She quietly recited verse after verse, something she did all day long.

Baby Boy got up from where he sat and went over to his mother, he patted her hands then gave her a cup still filled with the lemon tea he picked up off the table next to her; he had brewed it earlier and now was cool enough for her to drink. He helped her bring the cup to her lips and steadied her hand as she drank. When she was done, he wiped her mouth with a napkin, folded it and then placed it on the table. They only had each other, that's the way it had been since his father died of a heart attack 2 years ago; just the two of them.

The sound of a car driving by brought Baby Boy back to *reality*; he rushed over to the window and saw Percy's car as it pulled into the front yard. Miss Edna was back. He pulled the flannel throw over his mother's shoulders, kissed her on the cheek then made his way across the street to Rae's house.

Baby Boy knocked on the front door, loudly enough so that his presence would be immediately acknowledged. He could barely wait to hear how his friend was doing. Miss Edna peered through the glass and then opened the door, she looked solemnly at him, and then motioned for him to come inside. Percy had dropped her off and left. Her look made Baby Boy's heart sank.

"Raenelle's pretty beat up Baby Boy, but she's a fighter as we all know. The doctor says she will be ok, although it will take a while for her to be back to normal, but she will be ok."

Miss Edna tried to hold it together but as the words left her mouth, she began to cry, then she leaned on him. Unsure how to handle the situation, Baby Boy touched her shoulder gently. She soon contained her emotions and then continued to speak.

"Her eye Baby Boy, they're not sure if she will still see

from her right eye again; it was damaged pretty badly. They said the major blood vessels were busted and *things* were torn. I cannot think of all the details right now. I just know that her eye is in bad shape."

Baby Boy led Edna to the chair in living room; she had begun to shake.

"Baby Boy, do you know who did this to my baby girl?"

He took a deep breath; he remembered the look on Raenelle's face when he was asked that question the night before. For whatever reason unknown to him, she did not want him to tell her mother, or anyone else for that matter who had done such terrible things to her. He would keep her secret until she was out of the hospital and back at home. He needed to ask why she didn't want to tell her mother or anyone else who hurt her. Baby Boy could not keep a secret like that for long. Somebody had to be told eventually, those stupid boys should not be allowed get away with it.

"No ma'am, I just happen to be walking through them woods when I seen her laying there ma'am."

Baby Boy swallowed hard; he hated to lie, his mother would be angry if she found out; it was against everything her Bible taught. Besides, who would believe that he would be walking through the woods at that time of the night? It was late and that area was surely dark and dangerous. He was sure that Miss Edna would soon figure it out.

"Well Baby Boy, I'm going have to do my own investigating" Edna said. "I can't just let it be. Raenelle's Daddy is on his way from Virginia as we speak. Percy sent word as soon as he saw my baby laid up in that hospital bed."

Edna pulled a cigarette from her bag, Baby Boy, who at this time sat across from Edna listened intently to every word. He picked up the lighter and held it to the cigarette so that it could be lit.

Edna blew a puff of smoke into the air; she looked around the room not really searching for anything in particular. She didn't want to look at the boy while she smoked. Baby Boy hated the smell of cigarettes; it reminded him of his father and were the reasons why he died. Memories came flooding back; Baby Boy blinked and blinked until they disappeared. They were to be kept in the dark shadows of his mind and be forced back when they tried to come out.

"Rae can't see any more visitors until tomorrow Baby Boy, her Grams was given the okay to spend the night with her. Dr. Greene made the hospital put a little cot in the room so she could be there with her grandbaby; you know how she gets. God bless that Doctor Greene. You hungry Baby Boy, you ate?"

Edna got up and headed to the kitchen; it was obvious she was not sure what to do or say at this point.

"I'm not hungry ma'am; I had supper with my mother earlier."

Baby Boy stood up, a car had pulled up outside the house; he'd never seen this car around before.

"We'll I'm going to fix me a little something, I haven't had a thing to eat since last evening."

Baby Boy watched as a *dark figure* stepped out of the car, and walked up the steps.

CHAPTER TWELVE

The pounding on the door startled Edna; she dropped the pan she had taken out of the cabinet.

"Who in the hell is knocking on my door like that?"

Baby Boy stood silently and watched as Edna peered through the window.

"Oh Lordy, Ray? Ray is that you?"

She flung the door open. Ray stepped inside and immediately hugged Edna closely.

Baby Boy recognized him, he was Raenelle's father. He waited for Mr. Ray to say something to Edna, but Baby By realized that the man he looked a bit angry, and confused. Ray let go of Edna and then came a barrage of questions. He wanted to know when he could go see his daughter, how badly she was hurt, who had done it, and why. He went on to ask about her expected length of stay in the hospital. He asked if the police was looking into the matter and then said he would get justice for his child at any cost! He demanded to go see her but Edna assured him that it would be useless to try, they would not be let in at that hour. Raenelle needed to rest.

After the rapid questions and Edna's one-word answers, Ray finally calmed down a bit then turned his attention to Baby Boy, he looked at him suspiciously. Miss Edna spoke.

"Ray, remember Baby Boy, he found Raenelle and brought her home. Thank God for Baby Boy Ray; our baby would not be alive if he hadn't saved her."

Ray turned around to face the big fellow standing in the corner of the small living room. Baby Boy stood tall above him; the boy held out his giant hand and Ray shook it; he tried to remember how old Baby Boy was, it had been a while since he last saw him, he had grown ten times taller is seemed!

"Thank you Son, I thank you for saving my baby girl."

Baby Boy just shook his head; no words came from his mouth. He knew it was time for him to leave, he had to check on his mother for one thing, and he also wanted to give Raenelle's parents some privacy.

"Miss Edna, I'm going home now ma'am; you need me to do anything 'fore I go?"

He kept his eyes on the floor.

"You run on home now Baby Boy; I'll come get you if I need you. Thank you again."

Edna held the door opened as Baby Boy awkwardly bent down and went through; she closed and locked it behind him.

Edna looked at Ray; he took off hat and placed it on a hook on the wall in the corner of the room. He sat down and held his face in his hands; Edna lit another cigarette then walked over to him. Ray slowly raised his head and looked at the woman who stood before him. Behind the cloud of smoke he could see her face. She looked tired and distraught. The smoking had aged her even more than last time he had seen her; her beauty was hidden behind a mask of worry and a few age lines.

He wanted to tell her that she was killing herself slowly with every puff of that toxic smoke that she inhaled, but decided to leave that issue alone for the moment, he had to keep his focus on his daughter. Edna's smoking habit would be dealt with at another time.

"Edna, you know I have to handle this, I have to do something about this situation. Tell me what happened again Edna, I need to know more details regarding this incident, and I need a straight story from you. Tell me how my Princess ended up in the hospital. Go on, I'm listening Edna."

Ray clenched his teeth. Edna walked away from him; *this man* who sat in front of her. This was the same man, who left them for a military career, the man whom she missed and cried for from the moment he announced that he had made his decision to leave. The man who had her running to the window every time she heard a car drive up, thinking that he had changed his mind and returned to them; something she did for about a year after he was gone. This man whom she still loved deeply, whose daughter asked for him, missed him, and had cried for him every single day. It was she, Edna, who had to play the part of Mommy and Daddy when he left.

Initially, Edna had made up her mind to wait and she did so for the first 3 years but then she got tired of waiting. She decided that she didn't need him then and she thought about telling him that she didn't need him now, especially since she had gotten pregnant again on his first visit back. Because of stress and worry, she had lost the baby in her 4th month of pregnancy; his fault once again. Edna did not need any additional aggravation from his man.

She blamed him for not being there; if he were around to take care of their little girl then all would be well.

"Tell me what really happened Edna. What has happened to my daughter? Why was she targeted?"

Ray's tone was accusatory and judgmental.

"Ray, I told you that Raenelle has not spoken two good sentences since she was found."

Edna was not in the mood, not at that moment. She did not want to argue, all she wanted was to get her baby better, and back home. She wanted Raenelle right here where she could take care of her as her mother.

"Where was she going Edna, why did she end up in the woods? How did Baby Boy know she was there, and you didn't? That's what I'm asking Edna."

She remained calm. "Why don't we go see her early in the morning Ray? We can talk about all of the other things after that. Isn't seeing her the most important right now?"

Ray got up and walked over to the window, he looked at nothing in particular; he just stared into the dimly lit street and waited. Edna knew that his silence meant that he wanted his questions answered. She spoke slowly and softly; she figured that it was best to get it all over with now.

"I sent her to get me a pack of cigarettes down over at Dover's store Ray, I ran out of cigarettes and I asked her to run and get me a pack."

Edna paused. Ray said nothing, he just continued to stare out into the night.

"What time was this Edna, what time did you send a 15 year old girl alone to buy cigarettes when it was just about dark, Edna? You know how bad it is in that part of town."

Ray turned to face her, he looked taller and more powerful than she remembered. Edna blinked several times, then took the cigarette she was smoking and used it to light another. Her hand trembled; all night long guilt had plagued her; she blamed herself for Raenelle's condition. She had said nothing to Grams about her feelings, she could not bring herself to do it.

She thought about the dark path that led through the abandoned buildings in that area of Jessup where the store was located. She was so desperate for a smoke that she didn't think twice about the dangers; rather than go herself, she sacrificed her daughter's innocence for a pack of cigarettes. She was ashamed.

Raenelle had protested and had asked her to wait until the next day, but Edna insisted, and to stop her mother's nagging, Raenelle decided to go.

Her beautiful daughter was now laid up at the hospital, battered and bruised because of a *stupid* pack of cigarettes. Tears rolled down Edna's face and she let them flow.

"Don't matter now Edna, all I need to know is who put their filthy hands on my Princess."

The cigarette she was smoking was only half done, but she pulled another from the pack, held it with fingers that had slightly black tips due to years of chain smoking – she lit up once more. Smoke drifted in front of her face creating a temporary screen; a shield from Ray. He was staring at her with a look that reflected remorse, disappointment, pity and love; all at the same time.

"You want something to drink Ray; a cool drink would do you just fine in this heat."

Ray stood up, he walked over to Edna, she avoided eye contact.

"What happened to you Edna? Where is the woman I once knew?"

Edna shook her leg nervously and still refused to look at him.

"You left me Ray, you left us. We could've been together here in Jessup. We would've been ok; you, me and our children. We could've been ok."

She burst into sobs with a painful gasping sound from deep within.

Ray remained silent for a minute or two; he allowed her to regain her composure. He wanted to hold her, but his emotions were largely conflicted. He didn't see the need to repeat the same thing he had told her so many times before. Jessup was not for him, he needed more. Now was not the time to get into that anyway. He was here for his daughter.

"I am not leaving this town until I find out who touched my girl. I'm making my way to see her now Edna, it's up to you if you want to come along. I don't care if visiting hours are over" Ray took his hat from the hanger and walked through the door. He waited on the porch for Edna.

Edna stood up and she looked around at the room. It seemed empty; the house felt cold since the night before when Baby Boy walked in Raenelle's beaten body in his arms. Edna shivered a bit, the memory of seeing her baby girl's condition was too much to bear. She decided to go into Raenelle's room to find something familiar to take to the hospital, something that would love to have that would remind her of home. She looked through the door and signaled to Ray to give her a minute; he nodded. She returned to the small room that Raenelle shared with her grandmother.

The bed was still neatly made with Raenelle's favorite pink spread with yellow Daisies on the frilled edges. The pillows were placed against the wood headboard and her stuffed animals were lined perfectly against them. The table that doubled as her dresser and homework station had her hair brush, combs, hair bows, and creams. The room was neat and clean, Raenelle's basket of clothes was tucked away. Edna knew that her daughter took pride in her possessions, as meager as they were. She was proud of her. She picked up a stuffed Zebra and smelled it, it reminded her of Raenelle, and it had her smell – the scent of like roses lingered. She would take the this one, Rae would like that.

Edna picked up her purse from the living room table, threw in her lighter and another pack of cigarettes, and then motioned to Ray that she was ready to go. He walked out to the car ahead of her; she took a deep breath then turned and locked the door.

Ray sat stoned faced in the driver's seat; his jaw twitched, he was angry. Just as they were about to drive away, Baby Boy appeared. He startled them both when he knocked on the glass. Edna jumped.

"Good Lord Baby Boy! You trying to kill somebody boy?"

"Sorry ma'am" Baby Boy hung his head shyly.

"Well Son, if you have something to say then say it, we're just about to leave to go see Raenelle."

Ray peered at Baby Boy from the driver's side of his blue Rambler Classic.

"I, I have to tell you som'thing, Miss Edna, Mister Ray."

"Well go on Baby Boy, tell us."

"Miss Edna, I can't go on and not tell you what I know."

Baby Boy paused again.

Ray was beginning to get impatient.

"Well speak Son."

Ray almost yelled at the young man.

Baby Boy's bottom lip trembled as he began to speak

"I know who hurt Raenelle, I know who done this to her. It was them Truitt boys Ma'am, Lester and Eugene. It's them boys that you work for Miss Edna."

Edna looked at the huge figure awkwardly leaning towards the window of the car. She waited for him to say more. Ray's jaw twitched again, he was beginning to get further agitated; Edna knew that look all too well.

Baby Boy continued to speak.

"I was on my way back from the general store when I saw Raenelle, she was walking on the other side of the street from where I stood. She didn't see me but I saw that the pickup truck them boys drove was following her. I hid behind the old school building and watched. I wanted to call out to her but that Eugene Truitt is always telling me that he would hurt me if I he ever heard me say a word in his presence. Them boys thought nobody was around; they didn't know that I was near them dark buildings, so they pulled and dragged Rae into the truck. She tried to get away, but they slapped her Miss Edna, Mr. Ray. That Eugene slapped my Rae so hard she fell over. She hit her head hard on the side of that truck and all they did was laugh. I wanted to run out there and help her, Mr. Ray Sir, Miss Edna, but them boys don't like nobody to stop them, they have guns, they say it all the time. Rae tried to scream but Eugene covered her mouth, pushed her into the truck and then drove off into the woods. I followed them, ran as fast as I could."

Tears streamed down Edna's face, and Ray grabbed the steering wheel of the car with both hands, his knuckles turned white. Baby Boy continued on with his account.

"I followed the truck until it stopped; I left Momma's canned beans in the old building and followed them into the woods. I could hear Raenelle scream, but I was too afraid them boys would shoot us both, so I hid until they were done. I'm sorry I couldn't stop them ma'am, I wanted to grab them both and tear them apart with my bare hands, but you know how they Daddy is evil. He would surely throw me in jail. He would lock me up and then kill me if he found out that I had hurt his boys. I can't die Miss Edna, there would be no-one to take care of Momma. I'm sorry, I'm very very sorry."

Baby Boy still stared at the ground. His face wet with tears.

"It can't be the same Truitts, the sons of the people you work for Edna? Tell me it's a different family; say it Edna!"

Ray's gaze was fixed straight ahead as he spat out the words.

106

"Those bastards know that Raenelle is your daughter, our daughter, and yet they took away her innocence without conscience? Don't you wash their dirty drawers Edna; don't you clean up after them and their turned-up nose parents? Don't you take care of those spoiled knuckle-heads? Haven't you been wiping their asses since they were babies? They disrespected you and me by touching *our baby*. Do they think that you were grooming her for them? Why, Edna, why Raenelle? Why our little girl?"

Ray pounded his fist on the steering wheel after every few words that he spat out in anger. He seemed to have fire in his eyes when he turned to Edna and Baby Boy. He felt a rage that he'd never experienced before.

"I have to go back to Momma now, tell Raenelle that I'm sorry, but I just had to tell. She going be mad at me, but I had to tell."

Baby Boy repeated those two sentences until he disappeared around the corner. It was sad to see the big guy all choked up like that. Edna knew that he really cared for Raenelle; she was the little sister he never had.

"We're going there now Edna, straight to the Truitts. I want to get my hands on those two scums. I'm going to make them pay for what they did if it's the last thing I do in this world. They think because their Daddy is the warden at Georgia State Penn and knows high officials that they can do whatever the hell they want! They think they have the right to put their filthy hands on my daughter, and there will be nothing for it? Well I'll go to hell first before I let anybody get away with hurting my Princess. Forget reason! Forget anything they have to say. They will pay!"

Ray pulled the lever and the car lunged forward into the street. Edna's heart pounded, she knew Ray's temper, and she knew that once he set his mind to something there would be no stopping him. Just like when he told her about his decision to join the Marines, his mind was set and there would be no turning back. Edna had to make a decision this time around, she had to step in and bring calm to an already sad situation. There was no need to add fuel to the fire; she couldn't handle any other tragedy. She certainly didn't want Ray to get into any trouble that could land him in jail; that would be very easy for Jimmy Truitt to arrange.

It was well known that Mr. Truitt had guns; his line of work afforded him easy access, and at least three – a rifle and two pistols – were kept as his home. Every member of that that family knew how to shoot; Edna had firsthand knowledge since she worked as their housekeeper and knew the ins and outs of the household.

"Ray you need to go to see your daughter before you do anything foolish, the law will handle those boys."

"*THE LAW* Edna? Are you listening to yourself? Their father is *THE LAW*, he will protect those boys at all costs. Who was there to protect my little girl Edna? Who was there to stop those fools from raping her and beating her to near death? "

The sound of the Otis Redding '*I've Been Loving You for Too Long*' broke though the conversation. The song played for a minute before Ray finally spoke again.

"I need to see my daughter; you're right, I do need to go see my Princess, but God help me Edna, somebody is going to pay, you can bet on that."

Edna said nothing; she sat quietly and let the tears roll down her face. They drove through the streets of Jessup towards the hospital. Her life was not supposed to be like this. None of this fit the picture she had had in her head when she was a young girl. Her visions of a happy family did not play out in reality. She was supposed to be happily married with two children and Ray as her husband. Her teaching career was supposed to be a success; her life now was so far from that image.

Otis Redding continued to croon.

CHAPTER THIRTEEN

Lester kept his eyes on his food sitting on the plate in front of him; it grew colder by the minute. His brain was inundated with thoughts, they haunted him. He was still thinking about the stupid thing he had done with his brother. He had regrets but dared not mention them to Eugene. He thought about the plan to rid the body that night, he should have insisted that they throw her in the river.

He wondered how she found her way out of the bushes and got help. He was certain that she would have died in the woods; there was no way she could have made it out on her own. Damn that Eugene, he always wanted things to go his way, he had to make all the decisions regardless if they made sense or not. He prayed that anything left that could link them to the incident would be found when they went back later that evening.

Eugene watched as Lester swirled the mash potatoes around and stared blankly at it on his fork; the biscuit, something that he would have eaten 3 of already, had one bite. He had made several attempts to eat but it seemed that he was unable to. He knew that his brother was thinking about their plans for later; plans to go back to the scene, to that area of the woods in search of evidence.

Eugene was famished; he let nothing stop him from stuffing his face. He reached over and grabbed another drumstick from the tray, slapped some more potatoes on the plate, drowned it with gravy, and took another biscuit. The radio blared in the background; his father's doing, he insisted on turning it up full volume every time they sat down to dinner. It was his way of forcing them to listen to the news broadcast, and no-one dared to speak until it was over.

Eugene turned his attention back to Lester; he did not trust his brother so much. He wondered what he was thinking; he had to be up to something. He was more talkative earlier, seemingly careless. He had surely made a 180 degree turn from just a few hours ago. Eugene wondered if he had spoken to someone, if he had gone against their plans and told Sherriff Whitfield what they had done.

The Sherriff had mentioned that something had happened, although he never gave much details. Eugene wondered what the Sheriff really knew, more importantly he began to think that his brother had betrayed him or was about to.

"What's going on Son, why aren't you eating?"

Jimmy Truitt's monotone drawl broke through Lester's and Eugene's thoughts.

"I heard about that game you played today Son,"

Jimmy patted his younger son on the shoulder, an unordinary gesture for him, it was his attempt to show that he was proud of his boy.

"I am sorry I couldn't make it Son, I had trouble at work."

Lester gave a half smile. His father always had an excuse, there was never enough time to spend with his children; it had been that way since he could remember. His father's time was better spent running here, there and everywhere. Most of the time these running around episodes involved women but he was always *'at work'* according to him.

Pearl sat quietly and watched the interaction between father and son. She too thought about Jimmy's lame excuses for not spending time with his boys; bedding women was his favorite thing to do.

Some female or another seemed to always make it their business to bring their sob story to Pearl. Some even came to their home to make claims that Jimmy Truitt had had sex with them, impregnated them, or took advantage of them in some way or another. The harassment took place in town, at church or any random place. Some of the women even claimed that Jimmy made promises to release their husbands, boyfriends, or sons from the penitentiary if they performed some sexual act. They complained to Pearl when the arrangement failed in hopes of getting a reaction – she assumed.

Pearl calmly dismissed the claims in the face of the person complaining or who made the accusations; she would boldly state that she believed none of it. If that failed to turn them away, she would hurriedly walk pass the women especially if it was in a public place. When they showed up at the house, she would quietly ask them leave her in peace, or threaten to call the Sherriff. She never engaged in a verbal confrontation with any the women; her way was not to create a scene. She was determined to maintain her dignity, no matter the cost; her social status depended on it.

She stood by her man even when one of the accusers, a black woman, brought a child that was the perfect mixed version of her and Jimmy. The woman said that the child was her proof that what was being said about her and Jimmy was the truth; she pushed the little boy forward so that Pearl could have a good look.

Pearl responded by asking the woman to leave her property, she demanded that she take her bastard child with her; never to return. She never mentioned the incident to Jimmy; but he found out anyway and convinced Pearl that things like that should be expected; especially to a man in his position. '

"People will continue to make me a target" he proclaimed.

Jimmy Truitt had power, and he used his power as the warden of the penitentiary, for his own gain. He made promised to grant 'special' favors to anyone who was able to pay the right price. This included those who had husbands or boyfriends locked away to serve long sentences. They all went to Jimmy; they begged and cried.

'Please help me Mr. Truitt, I will do anything.' They would plead, and they did! He would deliver on some promises, but not all. An inmate may go from no recreation time to a sudden reprieve, or he may decide to let the guards overlook an infraction here or there. Jimmy knew how to use his position well. He had office visitors going in and out all day; his secretary knew when to hold his calls; she knew when not to disturb. He had many friends in the right positions: Judges, lawyers, and bail bondsmen; he was well connected.

Jimmy's ties with the Governor made his position that much more coveted; he had the ability to influence any decisions made with regards to the prisoners. If he wanted someone released early, all he had to do was make a request of the Governor; if he decided otherwise, same thing. Yes, he had power, and he embraced it! He was in a good place. Life was good. Never mind the rumors about children here and there – that could never be proven; even so he would deny it all to his last breath.

As for the woman who boldly took that child to his door steps, she had been kept at bay; eventually she got what she wanted. Jimmy decided that he didn't have time to deal with such matters and he didn't want to run the risk of having the child return to make claims later on either. He made the call to the Governor and let her have what she wanted. He released her worthless piece of a man.

~~~~~~~~

Lester waited for his father to continue to speak, he said nothing further; this signaled the apparent end of the conversation. Jimmy went back to focus on the meal before him and listened to the final few minutes of the news. He shook his head intermittently when he heard something he disagreed with or found to be of interest.

Eugene finished his second helping of food, waited for the radio announcer to say '*and that brings us to the end of the news report for this evening*', then asked to be excused from the table. Their mother, who had been quiet most of the evening, nodded at him.

Lester looked as his mother; he sensed that there was something troubling her, she didn't even insist that Eugene help to remove the dishes from the table; something she did almost every night. Lester followed his brother and asked to be excused from the table. He wanted a chance to discuss going back into the woods with his brother.

"You heard about what happened to Edna's daughter

Jimmy?"

Pearl scraped the food scraps from the plate and waited for a response from her husband. Jimmy lit his cigar, blew a puff of smoke into the air, and then replied.

"Yes, I heard what happened, she got herself in some trouble, probably went to be with some boy and it got out of hand. These young black girls get fast and hot too young. Edna asked you for money Pearl? Is that it?"

Pearl sighed, that was the way he thought all the time. Somebody always wanted money or some other help. Sometimes she wished that she could take his arrogance and shove it down his throat. Were it not for the privileges that came along with being the wife of the Warden of the Georgia State Penitentiary, she would have left him a long time ago; she was fed up with his nonsense.

After the first bastard child showed up at her front door; any other woman would have surely walked away; but being the ex-wife would not afford those dinners at the Governor's mansion, nor would it allow her to keep the titles of Secretary and Treasurer of the envied Velvet Ladies Socialite Group of Jessup.

She had come a long way from her want-to-be days; working hard to reach this place in her life. She was at the top of the game; the talk of the town when it came to her events and galas. She spared no expense to be the best. She held the crown. There was no way that she felt ready to give it all up.

"No Jimmy." Pearl finally responded to his question about Edna's need for money.

Both Eugene and Lester froze in their tracks; they waited to hear any mention of death, or a body. Any detail would help to answer some of their burning questions.

"Priscilla, the head nurse at the hospital, called me this evening; apparently she was brought in pretty beat up. They are not sure what happened, but they know she was raped, and she endured some cruel torture. One eye is badly damaged. It's sad that that happened to Edna's daughter. She is a good worker, that Edna".

"Well, we aint got no extra money to help, we pay her enough. If she need help we ain't got it."

Jimmy Truitt dismissed his wife. He continued to puff on his cigar while he listened to sports program on the radio. Whatever had happened to Edna's daughter was not his problem he concluded.

There was no remorse, no feeling, and no thoughtfulness for the poor girl nor for her mother. Pearl expected that, Jimmy was a real selfish man. She continued to pile the dinner plates on top of each other. Even though Edna had been with them for a while, she and Jimmy never really interacted. She supped that would be his reasons for being so nonchalant about the tragedy. He was not emotionally tied to Edna in any way. She sighed and continued with her chore.

From the corner of her eyes, Pearl noticed that the boys were lingering around in the sitting room; that was unlike them. Usually they would be gone after dinner – running around the streets of Jessup. They were just like their father, no morals, no feelings for anyone but themselves; well that Eugene mostly. Lester just followed suit because he wanted to be close to his older brother.

Pearl often wondered how such a *dumb* person like Eugene could have been born from her; there had to have been some mix up. The mid-wife delivered him right here in this house, so that was unlikely, but still, it was a mystery to her. He turned out to be a disappointment; perhaps she should have tried to hug him more when he was a boy.

Lester was just a little *'do boy'* for his older brother, he was not dumb academically; very smart – book wise – and a good athlete with a promising future.

Lester was very a talented football player – she had watched him play a few times. The whole town loved him, he was definitely the star of the team. Pearl prayed for her youngest son to make it. She hoped that he would use his brain along with his love of sports to get ahead and not stay in a dumb slump like his idle brother. Pearl still had a hard time loving her eldest child the way that she knew she should.

Pearl blamed their wayward behavior in part to the lack of guidance from their father. Eugene's misguided and juvenile delinquent attitude was to be expected anyway, he was totally ignored as a child. Jimmy never made an effort to spend time doing father/son things with him and the over doting on Lester stopped as soon as the boy turned 2 years old. Their sons were left to do whatever they wanted the only good thing was that they had each other. Still, Pearl felt that it was a shame that Lester allowed himself to be led like that. He denied it was so whenever she confronted him about it.

There were so many times that the boys got into trouble; Pearl lost track. She remembered when they were accused of stealing soda pop from the general store, breaking windows at the bookstore, or pulling the fire alarm at the church - stupid things like that were all orchestrated by Eugene, she was sure of it. Lester was not the type to plan such mischievous things.

~~~~~~~~

Eugene was twenty-one years of age; he decided to drop out of school a few months shy of his tenth grade education. His being in school was more of a headache to Pearl than his leaving. She grew tired of going to the school every other day to see the principal because of complaints about things that he had done, some trouble or another that he had gotten in to. At one point a teacher declared that he was just taking up valuable space in the class; she was right. Pearl made an attempt to continue his schooling at home but he proved to be too lazy and did not want to learn. She wore her patience to naught and so she gave up trying.

~~~~~~~~

"What are you boys up to?" Pearl asked.

They both looked at her apparently startled but neither answered the question.

"I believe your Momma asked you boys a question and I ain't heard no answer."

Jimmy puffed on the cigar, more smoke wafted through the air.

"We're going to meet a few of the boys in town".

Eugene replied, he always had an answer for everything. Lester looked at his fingers nervously; he said nothing.

"Alright go on then but make sure you are back home at a decent hour."

Jimmy waved the cigar as he spoke, the tip that was in his mouth looked wet; it disgusted Pearl.

Eugene was quiet this time; his father always gave

them a curfew but it didn't mean a thing. Most nights, when they returned home, he would be passed out in the sitting room or already in bed and had no knowledge of the time they came or went. He just spoke because he could; there was nothing of meaning behind his words.

"We'll be home soon Pops." Eugene stated.

He and Lester hurried out of the house and into his pickup truck.

"You need to pay more attention to what those boys do Jimmy; they roam around Jessup too much. It's likely they will fall into trouble and end up in that very jail that you oversee."

Pearl's words may have well fallen on deaf ears. There was no response from her husband. She gave the dishes a good washing, dried and then stacked them neatly in the cabinets. Edna had done a fine job arranging things in the kitchen; Pearl could find whatever she needed with her eyes closed. Tomorrow, she would send word to have Mahalia come to help out with the house chores since Edna had not shown up for work.

Mahalia's mother worked at the penitentiary and, according to Jimmy, asked if he could offer her daughter a job as a house cleaner. The girl was finished her secondary schooling but could not find work. Of course, Jimmy did not consult with Pearl; he just brought her home one day and announced that she would be assisting Edna.

Pearl didn't really care for her especially since it was rumored that Jimmy had had a thing with her mother. She began to come for a few days a week but those arrangements quickly changed and she showed up Monday to Friday like clockwork. It appeared that Edna was happy for the help especially with the cleaning. Pearl decided that it was pointless to object. Mahalia did as she was told without giving any trouble, and that was good enough for Pearl.

"Oh Pearl, those boys don't have an ounce of bad blood in them, they are just boys. Stop worrying." The words broke through her thoughts.

Jimmy continued to listen to the bluegrass tune blaring through the radio; he tapped his feet and puffed his cigar. The sports program had come to an end. Pearl shook her head, and after she ensured that the dining room and kitchen were cleaned to her satisfaction, she retired to the sitting room to continue her knitting. Jimmy would be Jimmy she concluded. It made no sense to try to have a decent conversation with him. Pearl silently hoped that her sons would return home in *one piece.* It was her prayer on most nights, and tonight would be no different.

CHAPTER FOURTEEN

As soon as he sat down in the pickup, Eugene punched his brother in the arm.

"What you do that for?" Lester asked, as he rubbed where Eugene had punched him.

"You need to stop acting so dumb Lester, you made it seem like we done something, standing there picking your fingers and all."

Lester didn't say anything but he wanted to scream at his brother and say *yes*, that they *did* do something; they left a girl who they thought was dead, in the woods. A girl they knew at that.

"What we going to do now Eugene? You heard Momma, that girl was found and she is laid up in the hospital. She is going tell that we did that to her Eugene. It's not like she doesn't know who we are. What are we going to do now Eugene? You have a plan? What's the darn plan? Sheriff Whitfield already came around asking us questions. What if he comes back?"

Fear gripped Lester, he didn't want to get locked up, and he had heard too many stories from their father about how the inmates were treated. Furthermore, as the son of the Warden, he would be an easy target for any cellmate.

"I don't want to go to jail Eugene; I don't want to be with all those men that Pops tells us about, I don't want to be there!"

"Shut your fucking mouth Lester, you're such a pussy. We ain't going to jail! No one saw us do nothing, and we goin' make sure that if that little bitch say we did anything, we tell them she's lying and then find her and put her away for good this time."

Lester knew that it wouldn't be as simple as threatening anyone or pretending that it would pass. He wanted to fix it but he wasn't sure how. For the moment, he made the decision to go along with his brother just so that Eugene wouldn't think that he was a wimp.

"Ok Eugene, ok."

Lester thought about football, and the possibility of being thrown off the team if the coach and school principal found out what he had done. He thought about his dream to play with a college team; one of those fancy colleges in the North would welcome him. Because of cowardliness, a foolish act, and the desire to prove to his brother that he was a man, his hopes and dreams had started to fade at a rapid pace.

The boys drove along the dirt road that led to the school playing field, the air was hot and the humidity was at a high; Lester could feel the sweat running down his back. Summer time in Jessup meant heat, lazy days and fun, but that summer looked bleak.

Summer days were long and everyone made sure to enjoy every ray of light the sun projected, down to the last minute. Lester had been looking forward to a good summer, he had planned to get a job at the gas station or tire shop with Eugene. He wanted to save his own money and perhaps take Jo-Ellen, the girl he had an eye on, to the movies or the hamburger joint to hang out. Now he wondered if any of this would still happen; he wondered if he would even get the chance to be around to do any of the things he planned.

Lester swallowed hard as he pictured some cold dark days ahead and they would worse yet if they were spent in jail.

They drove around town, not sure what to do for the remainder of the night. They had earlier decided that it made no sense to go into the woods; the girl was definitely not there anymore and it was too risky to attempt to find evidence they may want to discard. Eugene suggested that they listen to the talk around town and get information on the girl. The most important thing to him was to find out who found the girl. The answer would determine their next move.

The boys agreed and they drove by the bar just to see if any of Eugene's friends were there. Things were quiet in town that night and they decided to head for home.

After a quick shower and a bite to eat, Lester went to his bed and hoped for a restful sleep. His wish was not granted because his nightmare was the incident, image for image, dancing in his head in living color. He thought about the girl and the pain she had suffered; his nightmare was nothing in comparison to hers.

CHAPTER FIFTEEN

Football practice was over at 5:30, Eugene and Lester were supposed to go straight home afterward; their mother ordered them to do so, but as usual, they would disobey her orders.

Lester spotted brother seated in the bleachers; he drank from a bottle that was wrapped in a brown paper bag. There was no question that it was Moon Shine, that fire water that Eugene forced him to drink on many occasions, including the night of the incident with Edna's daughter. Lester hurriedly put away his gear, showered and went to meet his brother. When he met up with Eugene, Lester noticed that his eyes were glassy; he talked and laugh uncontrollably. There was no doubt that he was under the influence of alcohol.

"I'll drive Eugene; I can smell that liquor coming through your sweat; and your clothes look horrible." Lester was disgusted with him.

Eugene grabbed his brother by the shoulder and spun him around. Lester's heart raced a bit. He hoped that his brother would not attempt a confrontation; he was not in the mood.

"I love you Lester, you're my favorite little brother."

The words came in a slur, and with that trademark silly laugh. Lester knew that by the morning his brother would not recall uttering them. Eugene sputtered as he tried to keep his balance. Lester freed himself from his brother's grip and steered him in the direction of the parked pickup truck. He saw some stains on Eugene's clothes and realized that his brother had vomited and maybe even urinated on himself.

"We're going home Eugene, you need to get cleaned up, you smell bad."

More laughter and foolish chatter followed. They reached the parked pickup truck and Lester searched his brother's pockets for the keys.

"I don't have the keys Lester; I left them at the bleachers."

"How about you check your pockets Eugene? You always keep the keys there."

Lester carefully patted his brother's top pocket on his shirt and the ones on his pants as well; they were not in either of those places. Eugene continued to laugh as his brother continued his search. Finally he jiggled the keys in Lester's face. He had made several futile attempts to grab them but each time he got close, Eugene would move. After ten minutes of chasing him around the pickup truck, Lester decided to sit in its bed and wait until his brother came to his senses. He was tired of his foolishness.

When Eugene realized that he was running around by himself, he walked over to the truck. He drooled a little and almost spat on his brother has he spoke.

"Aw, you're no damn fun Lester; you know how to spoil a good time."

"Let's go home now Eugene its near nine o'clock, Momma will be worried."

"Worried my ass. Boy you know Momma don't give a damn about what time we come home, nobody gives a shit about us Lester, nobody! Our father doesn't speak to us, he shows no interest in what we do. He is the warden of the state penitentiary Lester, and I work at a dam gas station, pumping gas for the dumb fools in this county. Do you know how that makes me feel? And you – when was the last time you saw him at your games? Has he asked you anything about going to college? Has he Lester? That man can go to hell for all I care. And Momma, she ain't no better. She just pretends to like us, for appearances, that's all. I'm sick of both of them!"

When he was done with his ranting, Eugene held out the keys to his brother.

"Here Lester, drive! Let's take the back road home; I need to feel the fresh air in my face."

It seemed as if he had sobered up for a bit.

Lester took the keys and climbed into the driver's seat. He thought about what Eugene had said about their parents and had to admit that he was right. Their parents only pretended to care about them; they put on a good show for their important friends when it suited them, but other than that he and his brother were pretty much on their own. Although Eugene could be a dumbass most of the time, Lester was glad that they had each other.

Every time he thought about his father's lack of enthusiasm in his football achievements, Lester grew angrier. He had played several big games and had been named MVP in the majority of them but it meant little because his father's face was not amongst those in the crowd cheering him on. Lester craved the feeling of sharing a proud moment with his father; even a few words to let him know that he as happy that his son had followed in his footsteps, and had become a star athlete. He was always too busy. His job was more important.

Jimmy Truitt was just a selfish bastard, and Lester wished he had the balls to tell him to his face. He wanted him to know that he never made the effort, excuses and excuses were all that he gave. It pained him most when people came up to him to tell him that he played just as his father did when he was Lester's age.

'What did it matter'? Lester thought as he drove along the dark back road.

Not having the support of the man they all thought he emulated made it all seem like a waste. Lester took a gulp of the moonshine his brother handed to him. He had worked himself up to a new height of anger. He inhaled deeply as the liquid burned his insides. He wiped his mouth and took two more swigs. Screw Jimmy Truitt, that fool of a father. Eugene was Lester's hero, not Jimmy. Eugene had taken care of him ever since they were little and he would stay by his brother's side; even if it meant doing what he knew was wrong.

But the memories of what happened that night came rushing back, erasing everything else that he had been thinking about. He drifted back to the scene from the beginning.

~~~~~~~~

"Hey Lester look."

Eugene pointed to a young girl walking by herself; she turned around when she realized that a vehicle was behind her, and then stepped further unto the sidewalk.

"Hey it's Edna's daughter" Lester said to his brother.

"She's alone; why is she walking in these dark streets by herself?"

Eugene had an impish grin across his face.

"Let's just drive on Eugene."

Lester stepped on the accelerator.

"Nah Lester, you just slow down, let's ask her if she needs a ride."

Eugene tapped on the dashboard excitedly.

"Hey, hey you little girl you, you need a ride?"

The girl kept walking. She was a pretty little thing too. Always had her head in books, she would come to the house with her mother Edna sometimes and would sit quietly and read while her mother worked around the house. She never interacted much with them; just a quick hello or goodbye, nothing more.

Eugene was fascinated by the way she spoke when she had conversations with her mother; full of words he had never heard before and surely didn't know the meaning of. He loved to listen to her voice.

"Hey you little bitch, don't you hear me talking to you? Come tell me some of those fancy words you like to use, come whisper them in my ears."

Eugene drunkenly yelled out the window, the girl kept walking, she pace accelerated.

"Stop the truck Lester, no little bitch is going to ignore me."

Lester stopped the truck as his brother demanded. Eugene jumped out and grabbed the girl. She tried to fight and started to scream. She called out for her Momma and fought. Eugene slapped her as she clawed at him; she struggled to get free. She continued to fight as hard as she could.

"Let me go." Her screams turned into sobs

She pushed and pulled in an effort to get away. She was a feisty one; she refused to become and easy prey.

"Open the door Lester."

Eugene put his hand over the girl's mouth as he shouted his command at his brother. She tried to bite him but he managed to push her into the truck without her teeth making contact with his skin. Lester's adrenaline was at a high level, he was scared and aroused at the same time. And the alcohol he had had earlier was beginning to take effect.

"Drive Lester, drive the fucking truck. We're going to show this little girl how to respect us; we're going to teach her a lesson."

Eugene held the girl in a tight grip. She began to sob even louder.

"Let's hear some of those fancy words you always speaking now little girl!"

"Let me out of here, I want my Momma" was all she screamed.

Eugene ripped her dress, the buttons popped off

revealing her chest, and her perky breasts were now exposed. He felt his excitement rising, the effect of the moonshine was on full blast, and the sight of the young girl's bare breasts contributed to the high he felt. The girl continued to scream at the top of her lungs, but no one would hear; they were already driving through the dirt path that led deeper into the woods.

"Let me go you ignorant bastards! Let me out of this truck! Your father may be a big shot, but when my Daddy gets his hands on you both, you will regret this. Let me out now!"

Her screams and shouts along with her chatter became ear piercing; she twisted her body as she yelled. She refused to shut up.

Eugene punched her in the eye twice, "shut up, shut up" he yelled after each punch. He swore he had warned her several times before but she refused to comply. He had to show her who was boss!

The blows silenced her for a while; she put her hand over her eye and crouched. Eugene took the opportunity to touch her breasts, they felt nice and soft in his hands, he completely ripped the remainder her dress; he bent down and sucked on one of her nipples. The feeling of the soft flesh aroused him even more. He grabbed the bottle of moonshine that lay on the seat and poured some of it on her nipple, and licked and sucked again.

Lester looked over at his brother and the young girl several times but Eugene shouted that he ought to keep his eyes forward. The girl continued to struggle once more, she yelled out things pertaining to her father and tried to spit at Eugene. He covered her mouth with his and tried to stick his tongue inside. She tried to bite him, but he was too quick, he slapped her with the back of his free hand; she screamed and kicked with all of her might.

"Eugene, let's just turn around and drop her off."

Lester grew more scared, the girl's screams were doing something to him; they had penetrated his conscience. At this point they had gone deeper into the woods. He carefully maneuvered the truck in an area where campers were known to pitch their tents. He didn't want them to get caught by anyone. The thing they were doing was bad and they would surely get in trouble.

"Shut up Lester, just shut your mouth. We got her now let's just do it. Wasn't it you who told me that she was getting grown? Now is your chance, be a man for once you fucking little shit." Eugene said as he pinned the girl against the seat with his body.

Lester felt the heat rising in him, his blood had started to boil; he hated that his brother called him names, especially in the presence of a girl; a girl that he had watched grow up. The need to prove his brother wrong took precedence over reason, after all she was just the helper's daughter anyway; she didn't matter to him. Why should he care?

Lester parked the pickup truck between two trees and got out. Eugene pulled the girl by her hair and let her fall to the ground; she was cried hysterically and called out for her daddy. Lester and Eugene both laughed, the moonshine was almost all gone by now, just a little was left in the bottle.

Daddy? What Daddy? Where was her daddy? As far as they could remember he was away somewhere in the military or so Edna had said. He was nowhere near Jessup and he certainly couldn't help her at the moment.

"We got your Daddy right here you little cock sucker, bet you suck cock all the time don't you?" Eugene grabbed his crotch as he spoke, he struggled to undo the zipper.

The girl kicked wildly and fought as hard as she could, she became free for a second and tried to run. Eugene grabbed her and threw her to the ground, he kicked her hard in the stomach. The boys had their penises exposed and one tried to stick his in her mouth. She wanted to get away; she tried desperately to fight back. Lester felt sick, but kept up appearances for his brother, he kicked her too, but he did it with less force; his conscience crept in once more.

"Here Lester."

There was something shiny in Eugene's hand, it was the flask which held the remainder of what had put them into a drunken stupor. Lester grabbed the metal container of *liquid fire* from Eugene, he put it to his lips, held his breath and forced himself to take a swig of the last bit of the nasty liquid. Thank goodness it was done, he would surely throw up if he had to drink another drop. It burned some more as it trickled down his throat. He watched as his brother's body jerked back and forth as he raped the girl.

She lay motionless with her face buried in the ground. There was blood on her torn clothes; her hair was wild and entangled with dirt and bush. Eugene pulled up her skirt, and pulled her underwear down to her knees. His movements rocked her limp body. Lester threw the bottle into the bushes as Eugene signaled for him to take his turn.

He really didn't want to commit the act but he walked over to where the girl lay. His head felt light and for a moment his legs refused to move, Eugene giggled. Lester focused on the girl, she had stopped crying. Shit, he'd been watching her for a long time, he noted the changes in her body from that flat board chest to developing breasts, curves, and hips. The alcohol did its job and took control of his rational thinking ability. He had fantasized about what it would be like to feel her beneath him, and now was time to find out. He had only half of a sexual experience prior to this. One of the cheerleaders had let him touch her breasts, and finger her vagina in the locker room. He was worked up now...ready to go.

"Get off Eugene, it's my turn now".

The destructive fire blazed at its highest.

"Let's piss on her dead body Lester."

Eugene spoke as if this was a brilliant idea. He could hardly stand straight. He had had another turn with the girl after Lester and was trying to hold himself up.

About 30 minutes had elapsed since they had started the rape and torture. At this point, they had satisfied themselves to the point of exhaustion. They stood over her and urinated as if they were doing so on a trash heap. They laughed as their body fluid spilled onto her motionless body.

The girl had not moved, not even after the urine hit her raw flesh; visible cuts and scrapes covered various parts of her body.

"Lets' go on home now brother, you've proved that you are a man." Eugene slapped Lester on his back; he had done him proud.

Both boys finally agreed to leave the girl in the open with the hopes that an animal would drag her body off to another area of the woods. The idea of throwing her in the river was briefly discussed but leaving her in the open was thought to be best.

Eugene put his arms around his brother's shoulder and led him to the truck. Neither looked back at the battered girl who lay in the damp cold moss. They drove home in silence.

Inside, Lester felt like crap; guilt and shame invaded his mind.

CHAPTER SIXTEEN

Ray gazed at his daughter's swollen body. Tears rolled down his face when he saw his beautiful Raenelle. The bruises, cuts, and the battered look of his Princess was too much for him to bear. He blamed himself for not being there to protect her, he felt the guilt tug at the core of his heart. He clenched his fists and prayed for the time when he could get his hands on the Truitt boys, he would surely make them suffer. The pain would be one hundred times worse than what they had inflicted on his baby girl.

He willed his anger to subside; he made every effort to hide his emotions as he stepped closer to the bed where his daughter rested. He touched her hand gently, lifted her it to his lips, and kissed it. She stirred in her sleep. She slowly opened the uncovered left eye and tried to smile when she recognized his face. She looked relieved to see her father.

"Daddy" she whispered. Her voice sounded hoarse and husky.

Ray gently put his finger against her lips and asked her not to speak. He continued to stare at her and she fought to stay awake. However, the medicine took control again and she fell asleep once more. Grams and Edna watched silently as Ray continued to touch his daughter's bandaged head and face. The gauze and tape prevented him from being able to have a full view, but he was very concerned about her right eye. The swelling around that side of her face was suspect; he was no fool, he knew the damage was bad.

"Grams, what are nurses saying about Raenelle condition? Have they given you any updates? Has she been in an out of sleep all night up 'til now?"

Ray looked over the bandaged arrears of his daughter's body, but his focus returned to the one area that completely covered Raenelle's right eye.

"What about the bandages Grams, how long will they be on? Have they said anything about that? Tell me what you know."

His questions came like rapid fire, one are the other; he wanted answers. His baby's condition and prognosis were of utmost importance to him. He also wanted the real story surrounding the real story the ordeal. He remembered every word that Baby Boy; the boy had given his account of the abduction but Ray needed to hear his daughter say it with her with her own voice; he wanted to hear the words *'Eugene and Lester Truitt did this to me Daddy!'* Anyone could see that she had suffered a lot during the ordeal; he just wanted her to say their names.

Grams looked around the room then fixed her gaze on an open window. She didn't know how to break the news to Raenelle's parents. The doctors of various specialties had spoken to her earlier; they each explained that Raenelle would have to go through as she recovered according to their prognosis. Grams' training as a nurse was in full gear from the onset and she was well aware that her granddaughter would not be the same again. She had suffered tremendous damage both physically and mentally. She would need all the support she could get to help with her recovery.

It started to rain, and the wind had picked up as well. A breeze flowed through the room. The slight chill in the air represented the apprehension Grams felt; there was no getting around it, she had to tell them. The news would not be good, and it would only serve to heighten the anger that Ray was already trying so hard to control.

"They said she won't have good vision in that right eye, the doctors said she will have to wear a patch 'til she gets older." Grams blurted it out.

Her statement was slightly off, actually if was not quite true. The patch would be permanent; Raenelle's vision would never return. The damage to the eye was too severe, and there was nothing that could be done to save the eye nor retain her vision.

Edna burst into tears and buried her head in Ray's chest; the words her mother had spoken had just penetrated her brain.

Ray spoke.

"Now do you understand Edna? Do you see why I can't let THE LAW take care of this? They not only took my Baby's innocence, they took her sight, and God knows what else."

Ray's anger was more visible now; his voice was raised and Edna's sobbing grew louder as well.

Raenelle stirred in the bed, the elevated sound of her father's voice and her mother's cries had awakened her.

She groaned a bit and automatically reached for her right eye, she pulled at the bandage.

Grams rushed over and stopped her from taking it off.

"No, no Rae, leave that there sweetie. It will keep the air from going into your bruises."

Raenelle turned her head in search of her father.

"Daddy you're here, I'm so glad to see you Daddy."

It was as if there was no-one else in the room except her Daddy. She reached for him. Ray released himself from Edna's grip and took Raenelle's outstretched hand into his once more. Her nails were jagged, and there were cuts and bruises all over. Her recovery would surely take a long time and the total healing even longer; no doctor had to tell him that, he could see it for himself.

"Daddy's here Princess, I'm right here. I'm not leaving you ever again. I'm here sweetie." Ray held back tears as he spoke.

No father should have to see his daughter in this condition. Ray sealed his vow to ensure that the two boys suffered as much as his daughter did; it was a promise. When he was through with them they would understand the *hard* way. They would be taught that it was not ok to damage another human being – worse yet *his daughter*. They were walking freely, carrying on with their lives. Oblivious to her suffering now and the reminders she would have for the rest of her life. *They would pay.*

CHAPTER SEVENTEEN

Pearl cursed out loud. The flour she measured spilled on the kitchen counter and onto the floor. A sudden and heavy pounding on the front door had startled her. She wasn't expecting anyone this morning. She had been busy with her pastry baking for the *Young Women's Christian Fellowship* event that evening; time was limited; they had to be done at a specific hour. She didn't have time for company at that moment. Mahalia, who had taken on more responsibilities with house chores assisted her, she also stopped suddenly.

Three weeks had passed since the incident with Edna's girl. Pearl had promised to pay her a visit, but with her busy schedule it was hard to fit in the time to do so. Each time she made an attempt, she remembered that she had more pressing issues to attend to or needed to be at home to handle other personal matters.

Mahalia looked at Pearl as the pounding on the door continued.

"Should I get that Ma'am?" the girl asked.

She never looked Pearl in the eyes, she stared past her, as if she was afraid.

"Oh, I'll get it, you clean up the flour."

Pearl wiped her hands in her apron, then walked to the front of the house. She straightened a picture of her sons that sat on the mantle; they were babies at the time – so innocent and cute back then. She pulled back the curtain that covered the glass pane on the door; she saw a huge Black man, he stood and looked directly at her; Pearl's breath stopped.

'*What the hell...who was he*'?

She did not recognize him. She lifted her hand and motioned for him to wait. Pearl wiped her sweating palms in the apron. She spun around for a while not certain what to do. The boys were out, Jimmy was at work, and the gardener was off that day. She had no male figure around and the thought of facing this big strange man alone scared her beyond words.

"Ma'am I just want to talk to you."

The baritone voice came through the barrier that separated them. Pearl took a deep breath, and then decided to open the door. She thought it was best to find out what he wanted rather than ignore him; he did not look like the type who would just turn and walk away. She twisted the knob and through a small crack, asked who he was and what he wanted.

"I am Raenelle's father; you know who Raenelle is don't you?"

The man looked her dead in the eyes; she opened the door wider.

"Of course, I know who Raenelle is. How is she coming along, how is Edna?"

Pearl stepped through the door and onto the porch, she felt a little relieved that the man had mentioned a familiar name but she still wondered why he was at her house.

"My daughter is still suffering, and she will suffer for the rest of her life, she lost her vision in her right eye."

The man stood motionless, he told her these things without a lead up, as if she should already know about them.

"Well that is very sad, very sad indeed. She is such a beautiful girl."

Pearl wasn't sure what to say. She looked at her Chrysanthemums, the garden looked great; the flowers were in full bloom, and the gardener had outdone himself with the design that year.

She waited and wondered if there was something she should say or do. She did not know what he expected of her but one thing for sure was that she had to return to her baking.

She wanted to ask if he came by to give a report on his daughter's condition or if Edna had sent him to borrow money. She concluded that Jimmy's suspicions were right; these people wanted something; money – most likely.

"Your boys did this to her. Did they tell you that?"

She heard the spoken words but they didn't make any sense.

*'Did he just say that **her boys** were responsible?'*

Was that what she just heard?

"Excuse me, Mr. Whomever you are..."

He looked at her, his hat clutched in his big hands – then replied.

"It's **Mr. Porter**, Ray Porter."

His gaze remained fixed.

She felt uncomfortable but resisted the urge to show it. She refused to be intimidated by this stranger.

"Mr. Porter, you must be mistaken, I have two good boys, they would not hurt anyone, especially not your daughter. Edna works for us for God's sake. Who told you that lie? By the way, what proof do you have of that ridiculous insinuation?"

Pearl wished that Jimmy was there at that moment, he would handle the idiot who stood there and spoke lies about their boys, and blatantly so at that.

"You should ask them about it Ma'am. You ask your boys and hear what they have to say."

"I don't have to ask them a thing mister man, they are good boys."

"Again, it's Mr. Porter."

"So what do you want huh? Money? Is that why you are here?"

The man looked at her angrily; his stare became more intense and penetrating; his tone grew sharp.

"I don't need your money. What I need and will get is justice for my daughter."

He said this in a matter-of-fact manner.

"Are you threatening me Mr. Porter? Do you know who my husband is?"

Pearl began to tremble, angry at the stranger who implied that her sons had done this thing so horrible and wanted them to pay. She wished again that her husband would hurry home.

"Frankly Ma'am I don't give a damn who he is, the fact is your sons raped my daughter and left her to die in the woods. Do you know that she is just 15 years old?" What on God's earth could she have done to deserve such a thing?"

Pearl trembled a bit. What was she supposed to say? How could she end the encounter and get the man to leave? She wanted him to go. There was nothing she could say to him. Did he expect her to say ok, my sons did this? She was ready for him to get off of her property.

Jimmy's car drove slowly over the gravel in the driveway. Having heard the sound of tires as they ran over the chipped pieces of rocks, Pearl and Ray turned towards the noise, both reacted at the same time.

Pearl welcomed the sound and the sight.

"Well, Mister Porter, my husband is here now, you can tell him what you just told me."

Pearl hurried down the steps and rushed to greet her husband, she could feel Ray Porter's eyes as they burned holes in the back of her head. She felt protected now; her husband had arrived. There would be nothing to be afraid of. As Pearl got to the car she spoke to her husband almost in a whisper.

"Jimmy, this here is Ray Porter, he is the father of Edna's girl."

Prior to that day, they had never met him, but Edna did mention him to Pearl at some point or another over the years. Pearl could not remember the details of the conversation, but she was sure that there was something said about his whereabouts. It seemed he was absent from Edna's and the child's life for a long period of time.

Jimmy eyed the man; he stood tall and commanding on his porch.

"What can we do for you Mister?"

Jimmy took his hat and jacket from the back seat of the car and closed the door; the tall man walked down the steps and met them in the walkway.

"It's Mr. Porter, and I'm here because your two sons raped and almost killed my daughter."

Ray got straight to the point with Jimmy Truitt as he had done with his wife.

Jimmy, squared his shoulders and pulled at the suspenders that were connected to his pants. The man did tower above him but he was about to let Mr. Porter know who was boss around these parts, and more so, of this property.

"Look here mister..."

Ray interrupted Jimmy.

"It's Mr. Porter, again."

"Well you listen to me *MISTER* Porter; you must have the wrong information 'cause my boys for sure ain't raped nobody. And they especially wouldn't rape Edna's girl. You should go back to where you came from and get the proper information, *MISTER* Porter."

Jimmy started to get angry.

What the hell did this man think? Did he believe that he could just show up and accuse his sons of such a thing unimaginable? He, Jimmy, was the warden of the state prison, if there was any crime committed that involved his sons he would have known, the Sheriff would have told him right away. As a matter of fact, Jimmy saw Sheriff Whitfield just the day before and there was no mention of any investigation involving his boys. He only mentioned that the girl had been badly beaten, and that was it. No suspects and no investigation.

"Well Mr. Truitt, Mrs. Truitt, I am sure you think your boys are innocent, I don't blame you, but I know what was told to me and I believe it. I have seen my daughter's beaten body and scarred face. I came here to ask for an explanation as to why they chose to hurt her the way they did, and to get justice for my child. Her mother takes care of those boys of yours, and has done so since they were young. Both of you stand here acting like they are so well-behaved and precious. I've heard of the many troubles those two have gotten into. Everyone in the town knows their character."

Ray shook his head as he stifled the rage which he truly felt, he then continued to speak.

"Somehow I expected that response and reaction, however, heed my warning. I will get justice for my daughter. Raenelle deserves it!"

Ray tipped his hat as he walked past Pearl and Jimmy; he got into his car and drove away; a trail of dust was left in his path.

"What will you do about this Jimmy? This man walked onto our property and made those horrible claims about our sons. Tell me Jimmy, what do you plan to do?"

Pearl was visibly upset, her face was flushed. She hoped that this would be the time that Jimmy stepped up as a father, it was his opportunity to show that he cared about his sons. If he cared at all, at this point in the lives of their children, he would put them ahead of himself.

"Calm down Pearl, I'll take care of this. Where are the boys now?"

Jimmy was not in the mood for a soap box episode from Pearl at that moment; he intended to get to the bottom of the matter perhaps just to shut her up.

He waited for her to answer.

"Lester is in school and Eugene is at work as far as I know Jimmy."

Pearl looked at her husband in disbelief. How could he not know where his children were at that hour of the day? Was he in his right mind?

They walked into the house; Mahalia had continued to make the desserts. The sweet smell of fresh baked pastries wafted through the air but Pearl was too distraught to notice. Mahalia was capable and enough sense to finish up. Pearl was relieved but she said nothing to the girl. Her main concern was that the social event would come off without a hitch. She would receive all the praises, the ultimate compensation for her hard work.

"Jimmy we can't have this man walk around and talk nonsense about our boys. Tell me what you plan to do to stop him."

Pearl gave serious thought to her reputation among the upper-class ladies – the socialites. If her boys had anything to do with the confusion – the mess – about Edna's daughter, it would create a rippling buzz that would be sure to disrupt her life. She would have no such drama and controversy taint her image.

Without answering his wife, Jimmy picked up the phone and dialed the number to the Sheriff's Office, an officer answered.

"Jessup County Sheriff's office; Officer Harding speaking."

When Jimmy identified himself as Mr. Truitt, Warden, his call was immediately transferred to the Sheriff Whitfield's line. The Sheriff picked up the phone on the first ring.

"Sheriff Whitfield here."

The Sheriff choked on the words and a bout of hacking cough followed. He made a promise to himself, for the thousandth time, that he would see the doctor and get medication to help relieve the retched infirmity. He had made and cancelled several appointments with Dr. Greene to help find the cause of his phlegm producing problem, but the time was never right. One excuse was that it would be time wasted since source was obvious. Doc would only tell him that he needed to stop using his snuff and that, as a solution, was not even an option for the Sheriff.

The cough was just an occasional interruption and at times came in quiet handy, he concluded. He had already decided that he'd bring on another bout if Jimmy got on his nerves at any point during the call. That would cut short the conversation and Jimmy's babble.

"Sheriff, this is Jimmy Truitt, I need to come to your office as soon as possible; we need to discuss a serious matter."

"Sure Jimmy, come on down any time. Do you want to tell me what this is about first though?"

Sheriff Whitfield coughed again.

The Sheriff had a good idea regarding the nature of Jimmy's call but he played along. Earlier that week, he had gone to Dr. Greene's office and had received details on the condition of the young girl who was found in the woods. Doc contacted the Sheriff after having driven the child and her family to the hospital. He gave a good account of the girl's injuries; noting that they were severe, and that permanent damage was certain. When Sheriff Whitfield asked if she had made any mention of who had committed the despicable act, the Doc stated that Baby Boy, the young man who had found her knew the details of that. Dr. Greene confirmed that did not suspect that the young man had anything to do with the incident. Sheriff Whitfield made careful and detailed notes.

Following his conversation with the doctor, the Sheriff made a trip to the hospital in an attempt to see and speak with the victim. The nurse in charge and the girl's grandmother advised him that she was in no condition to be questioned; he would have to return when he received clearance from the treating physician.

Ida May, whom the Sheriff knew well, cried as she begged him to find the culprits that ruined her granddaughter's life. The Sheriff promised to do his best to find the perpetrators and bring them to justice. The family deserved it, he assured. A few juvenile delinquents came to mind as possible suspects, but the Sheriff kept that list to himself; proper investigation would be carried out and the guilty party or parties would be dealt with.

Jimmy Truitt's voice came through the receiver.

"I'm on my way now Whitfield."

~~~~~~~~

Jimmy hung up the phone, picked up his bunch of keys, and walked towards the front door. Pearl had stood by waited on him to tell her his plans.

"Go get the boys Pearl; I don't want that crazy bastard coming back here to try anything stupid. Go get them before he gets to them; he's Edna's man, she may tell him things to make it easier to put his hands on them. Go before those boys of yours do something else to stir up more trouble. God knows how the number of times I've had to ask Sheriff Whitfield to keep them out of jail, especially that Eugene. I'm getting pretty sick of their stupidity."

He slammed the door as he left.

Pearl stopped for a minute. *'Did he just say before they do something else?'* She tried for a moment to convince herself that she'd heard wrong, but she knew that the words were real. What she really wanted to do was to tell Jimmy that the boys turned out that way because he made no time to be a real father to them; that he - Jimmy was a self-absorbed idiot!

She grabbed the keys to her car and left the house. She called out to Mahalia to put the pastries in containers and to finish up. She closed the front door as she left.

CHAPTER EIGHTEEN

The first few days following the horrific incident were hell for me. I hardly slept; I tossed and turned and would wake up screaming. Most times I would be drenched with sweat; and would tremble uncontrollably. I constantly called out for my Daddy.

I had to be sedated twice because some of the episodes would bring me to the point of hysteria. Daddy and Momma took turns staying up throughout the night. They would quickly be at my bedside whenever I called out for them. Things got worse for me when they broke the news to me that I would not be able to see from my right eye. After that I refused to eat, and sometimes I barely spoke. I had to be given nutrition intravenously because of refusal to eat.

When I was finally released and got to our house, the real worries began. My family thought that I would get out of I slump being in familiar surroundings and speed up my recovery but I slipped deeper into depression. I still could not eat.

After a few days, Daddy suggested that they take me back to the hospital but Momma and Grams refused; they kept vigilance day and night, taking turns to comfort me when my nightmares kept me from sleeping. Daddy hugged me every time he got the chance to; the guilt he felt of not being there to protect me, especially on the night that I was brutally raped, was overwhelming for him. I heard him say it when he spoke to Momma. He had promised to protect me on the day I took my first breath; to care for me at all cost. He said that he felt like a failure. He regretted that he lived in another state; he blamed all this on himself. I wanted to tell him that it was ok, but the words would not come out. I knew that his chest felt heavy and that his blood boiled. He swore to make it up to me.

~~~~~~~~

As he sat in his car a short distance from the school, Ray wondered if his daughter would be able to return there to continue her education. She had had a bright future, she was intelligent beyond her years, and spoke of her dreams to become a marine biologist. He was proud of her accomplishments; she had received several academic awards and was always the top student in her classes. Now, thanks to those young ingrates, going back to school, if and when that time came, would be tough for his daughter.

He thought about her eye. What young girl wants to walk around with a patch over her eye? How would she react when told that she may not be able to bear children, and all through no fault of her own? Those thoughts only angered him more.

Ray spotted Pearl Truitt, she hustled into the building; just as he planned he had put fear in them. She was there to protect her precious son's life; she had come to get her boy. He shook his head. Good! He thought, they took his warning seriously; he put his car in gear and then drove away. He knew that the other boy worked at the service station, neither of the two was hard to find; easy targets – just like they viewed his Raenelle.

Ray didn't give a damn about Jimmy Truitt and his position as the Warden, all he knew was that if those boys did not pay for the damage they did to his daughter through the law, they would pay by the method he chose. Anyone who knew him would choose the first. When he went into military mode he was a force to be reckoned with and nothing pretty ever came out of that.

There was good reason why Ray chose to live in Virginia. It was not an easy choice having to live so far away from his daughter, and he had only arrived at the decision to do so after much burdensome anxiety. The constant frustrations regarding the personal stagnancy drove him to make that move. The same old feelings persisted with him living in Jessup- there was not much for him to do; he had to leave in order to create a better life for himself and his child. He had made that promise even before she was born.

~~~~~~~~

When Ray told Percy about his impending move and what he intended to do, his friend readily understood and gave his support. Percy was well aware of Ray's frustrations. He also knew that it was a hard decision for him to make, since his daughter and Edna would have to stay behind in the interim.

Both men had served their duties in the Marines with merit, but returning to Jessup after their tour was over, didn't guarantee any good jobs or growth prospects. Their employment options were the mills or some low paying security job; the latter of which were scarce in those parts.

Percy decided to invest some of the money his parents had left in a little bar in town. It did well enough so that he did not have to seek employment elsewhere. His friends in Jessup supported him, and soon the bar turned into the 'happening' spot. It was where his own people could hang out and have a fun time without being harassed by the 'authorities'.

Ray had already made contacts in other states during his quest for suitable jobs; he desired a job where he could use his skills as an ex-Marine; something that was worth his while in all areas. He refused to settle back into the same routine he had before he left for the military.

~~~~~~~~

It was a Friday night; Ray and Percy had gone down to the bar; they usually hung out together on Friday and Saturday nights. Ray felt comfortable at Percy's Place; he could listen to the juke box or a live band, shoot some pool and eat – all in one spot. That was the best way to relieve stress and have a good time; it was their thing, *it was everybody's thing*. Sammy, the barkeep Percy had hired, kept the drinks flowing; the pool table held heated games – men would bet half their week's salary on a single shot; the norm on payday.

Ray was not so foolish, he had a daughter to support, and besides, making his way out of Jessup also required that he save and be prudent with his spending.

Big Joe and Willy battled each other at pool table number 3, and as usual, there was tension in the air. Ray scoped the joint and noticed two men sitting at a corner table at the far left, almost to the back. They were not regulars; they were dressed in black trendy suits – dead giveaways. One looked like he could be around Ray's age, and the other man was older, and rather distinguished looking for a place such as the bar. They turned to look at the pool game on and off. It was apparent that they were very interested in Willy.

Ray kept his eyes on the pair; they drank slowly and paid after each drink; an indication that they would leave in haste at any moment.

When Willy left the pool table, seemingly to take a piss, one of the men got up and followed; Ray got up from the stool where he sat and walked in the same direction. The restrooms were at the back of the bar; just down a short corridor. Willy went into one of the stalls to relieve himself, oblivious to the fact that he had been followed.

The music from the juke box played loudly, and people chatted and laughed. There was noise all over as men yelled at each other while they engaged in the various games scattered about the joint. There were dart boards, card games, chess, checkers, and pool tables. They cheered and fussed at each other; but no one ever got out of control.

Women flirted and danced at the tables, trying to get the attention of the men, or at least score some cash. Action took place in the spot, all had a good time. The place was truly abuzz.

The man who followed Willy waited outside the door of the stall that he had just entered. Ray pretended that he needed to use the facilities and took up position in line; he kept back about two arms lengths of the stranger.

"The other stall is free" the man said.

"That one is out of service, been that way for a while." Ray quickly answered back.

He kept his eyes on the door, waiting for Willy to come out.

Ray could tell that the stranger packed a *piece* under his jacket, his heart began to race; adrenaline flowed. The gun may mean *bad news;* the situation just did not look good, and Ray sensed that Willy was bound to face grave danger.

"What's your name?" I've never seen you in these parts before."

The man stared at Ray; he did not respond.

"Yo Willy, how long you going to be in there man?"

Ray yelled loudly and moved closer towards the stall. The toilet flushed and then the door of the stall swung open. Willy stepped out, he was about to speak but when he noticed the stranger, he kept quiet. The unknown man shuffled; he adjusted his pants and unbuttoned his jacket.

"Who's your friend Ray?" Willy asked.

"Go on now Willy, he's none of your business." Ray replied.

The man put his hand inside his jacket. Ray stood between him and Willy. Willy sensed that there was something odd, so he backed away and made his way to the center of the action; he returned to his pool game. He had enough sense to know that he shouldn't stick around to get an answer.

The man said to Ray, "You're standing in the way of me making some money mister."

He looked Ray up and down. It may have been his height and built that intimidated the stranger but Ray noticed that the man made no attempt to go after Willy.

"I say keep your hands out of your jacket, and your

business outside of this establishment, and we'll be alright."

Ray squared his shoulders and stood tall; he wanted to make sure that the unspoken part of his message was being heard loud and clear. He was not someone to be messed with.

"You need to mind your own business." The stranger said.

As the man tried to brush past Ray, his path was blocked. Percy, who had been keeping his eye on Ray and the strange man, had hurried to where his friend stood; when he reached the pair, he stood and stared without saying a word. The man shuffled from one foot to the next, he unsure of what to do. His partner, the older man, had kept watch also, but he didn't want to draw any unwanted attention. One thing he knew for certain was that the big guy alone, by his sheer size, could take him down. The picture he created in his mind caused him to think for a moment. He got up from his seat and walked over to his companion and the other two men. Then he spoke.

"Excuse me, my apologies, but are you two gentlemen looking to make some *real* money?"

Neither man answered but the man continued with his proposition.

"I would like to make an offer to both of you. I'd rather not about it here. If you're interested, we can go outside where it's more private."

"We can hear just fine right here" Ray said.

He was already agitated, and it showed. He folded his arms, revealing the definition of his huge biceps even more.

"Ok then, we can talk here."

The older man knew military men when he saw them. He introduced himself and went on to tell Ray and Percy about his private investigating firm. He gave some details about the training, the skills needed, and the *great* salary that could be made. Ray's curiosity peaked, but he did not show it. He thought about his military training and the possibility of putting it to good use after all. He would have to verify and validate the claims the man had made but it could be his way out of Jessup once and for all.

After an impressive *sales* pitch, the stranger then explained that the job would require relocating. If for no other reason, Ray was ready to jump at the opportunity. His desire to move out of Jessup and find new pastures could not be suppressed.

The man introduced himself as Phillip Perkins, he gave business cards to the pair, and asked them to get in contact with him if they wished to join his employ.

"What is your business with Willy?" Ray finally asked.

"Let's just say you saved your friend; I have three other associates who would've come in here the moment I gave the signal. It's fine now though; if you decide to come join us, then Mr. Willy's slate will be wiped clean – he owes some people money and they hired me to collect".

The man looked about the establishment then continued.

"You gentlemen think about it, you could be making a great investment in your future if you make the right choice. Don't forget that you'd be saving your friend's life at the same time."

On that last note Phillip Perkins tipped his hat and left;

his associate followed close behind.

Ray thought about Percy; he had his business establishment which was doing rather well; however, Phillip Perkins had given Ray something to think about. Leaving Jessup was all he wanted at this point; he wanted to give his daughter a better life and a brighter future; one beyond the confines of their town. The need consumed his thoughts at night; it weighed heavily on his mind when he hung out with his daughter; watching her play or just spending quality time with her. She ignited the ambitious fire in him; and was his drive to achieving the best that life had to offer.

Four weeks after scrutinizing and *playing* with the business card; reading it, and questioning if it would be the right opportunity for him; Ray decided to make the call.

From their phone conversation, Ray discovered that Phillip Perkins was even more than he had first thought. As it turned out, Mr. Perkins was a wealthy man who owned quite a few lucrative businesses. Not only did operate a large private investigating and security company, which included bounty hunting and bail bond services, but he was also a successful realtor, transport specialist, and a bit of an influential politician in the making. The man was a tycoon of sorts.

After he bade Raenelle and Edna goodbye, and promised to have them moved out to Virginia as soon as possible, Ray made his way to Virginia. The meeting was to have initial discussions with Mr. Perkins, so see first-hand what he was up against. He fell in love with the place at first sight. He felt a good vibe from moment he arrived. He was shown around, introduced to business associates, and helped to get settled; Mr. Perkins had arranged it all.

Ray was anxious to get to work, he busied himself with

learning all that he could about his new job. He studied all
the materials, and took all the required tests; in a short
time he obtained the necessary licenses and became an
official Private Investigator/Bounty Hunter. He felt good.
He could put his plans in motion to have his family possibly
join him sooner than expected. This was perfect and for
once, he felt in charge of his own destiny.

His goal had been to take Edna and their daughter out
of Jessup, but he first needed to get himself settled, and get
his finances together. It would take money to relocate his
family and maintain them once they got to Virginia.

Although the relationship between him and Edna had
grown strained after he joined the military, Ray never had
interest in any other woman; many had tried, but they
could never hold a candle to her. There was no one like his
Edna; the thought of her still stirred up feelings inside.

It was sad that she was so bitter about his decision to
join the Marines. He could not blame her though, he had
left when their daughter was still a baby, and in addition to
that, she had lost what would have been their second child.

She had found out that she had gotten pregnant after
he returned to Jessup from first tour of duty in the
Marines. He was told the news after his time off ended and
he was shipped out. Once more, he would not be around to
be her comfort and support. He could certainly understand
her resentment towards him, but he intended to make up
for it in every possible way.

CHAPTER NINETEEN

Ray maneuvered his car and pulled up to one of the gas pumps at the service station; he switched off the engine and then got out. He spotted the Truitt boy; he recognized him, he resembled his arrogant father. He looked busy as he changed the oil in someone's vehicle. The boy was totally oblivious to everything and everyone else around. He just whistled away as he wiped his grimy hands on a dirty rag. He was in a happy mood it seemed, just going along his merry way. The carefree life may be something that would never be for Raenelle; who knew if she would ever be that way again. All the uncertainty was because of that worthless piece of shit.

Ray walked up to the door of the service station convenient store, the bell chimed as he stepped through. He had to bend a bit; the place was not built with men of his size in mind. He looked around at the tiny room; there were all types of items stacked on the shelves, from bread to shoe polish. The place seemed too small to stock so many items, there was hardly any room to walk around, and it was even more difficult for him.   He picked up a pack of bubble gum, Raenelle's favorite; she loved to chew the gum and then attempt to make huge bubbles. He smiled as he remembered the look on her face when she accomplished the feat. He put the item on the counter and informed the skinny pimpled face boy behind the wire cage that he needed ten dollars' worth of gas. The boy took the money without acknowledging that he had heard Ray's request.

"Hey Eugene, somebody needs gas," the boy yelled pass Ray.

Outside Eugene had already made his way to the gas pump and had unscrewed the gas tank on the car. Ray walked slowly toward him; he could hurt him right now if he wanted to, he could just snap his neck with one motion.

"Sure is hot today."

Ray had walked slowly to the car, his voice carried in the wind. He stopped just as he got within earshot and stood directly behind the boy.

"I thought about going fishing in the river through those woods but I heard that a girl was found there, raped and near dead. Not too sure about walking into such a place, you never know what's lurking. What do you suggest? Think I would come into some danger or something like that little girl I heard about? Heard she was pretty beat up; must have been some kinda night for whoever did such things to her."

Eugene lost his grip on the gas nozzle for a split second; the liquid ran onto the car and spilled over to the ground. He regained his composure and turned to look at the man that had spoken. The stranger towered above him, he made Eugene feel like he was 3 feet tall.

"I don't know nothing 'bout that Mister."

Eugene took the oily rag from the back pocket of his soiled overalls and attempted to wipe the side of the car. The rag created a slick streak, it created a bigger mess. He looked at the man, there was a darkness on his face.

"Strange that you haven't since that is all the talk around town; but hey, we don't all pay attention to everything around us. Aint that right son?"

Ray looked directly into Eugene's eyes; there was something there, he figured that is was most likely a fear the boy had never known before.

"I don't know nothing 'bout that nor do I know about that girl."

Eugene finished filling the tank, replaced the cover and turned to walk away.

"I'm *that girl's* father, Raenelle – that's her name. I will make sure that whoever did this to her pays for it. Just in case you know who did, you can tell them I said that, and deliver the message the same way I gave it to you son, the same way I gave it to you."

Ray got into his car, turned on the ignition and left Eugene standing in the dust that had stirred up as he pulled out of the station. He had gotten the desired reaction, he had planted a seed of panic in the boy's mind. Ray hoped that he would deliver the message to his stuck up and arrogant parents.

CHAPTER TWENTY

Eugene willed everything inside his stomach to stay down; he watched the car until it disappeared down the road. He had already observed the muscular size of the man as he stood beside him while he pumped the gas, but the minute the man identified himself as the girl's father, the stranger seemed to take on an even larger *tanker truck* built.

Eugene managed to uproot himself from the spot where he stood after the man left and ran into the building.

"I'm leaving early today man; I have an emergency." He yelled at the kid in the convenience store.

He grabbed his cap, then picked up his keys and ran to his truck. His heart raced as he drove haphazardly down the road and away from the station to his house. He could hear the man's words ringing in his head.

'I will make sure that whoever did this to her pays for it.'

"Shit, shit!" Eugene yelled as he banged his fist against the dashboard, he thought for a minute.

Suddenly he remembered his brother Lester, he was not as strong as Eugene and would crumble under pressure. He wondered what Lester's reaction would be if that same man went to find him and asked the same questions. Eugene turned his truck around and drove towards the high school instead; he had to get to his brother before the girl's father did.

As he pulled up to the school, he recognized a car parked in the lot, it was his mother's. He pulled up next to the vehicle, looked around for a moment and then got out of his truck. He touched the hood; it was still warm; she could not have been there too long.

He had no plans what to do nor did he know what to expect so he got back into the truck and waited. If his mother emerged from the building with his brother in tow then he would definitely know that something had happened at home or at the school. His mother didn't just show up for spot checks, she never did that. Something had to have happened and he was curious to find out what it was. He wondered if the man, who said that he was that looking the person who hurt his daughter, had been around or had caused some stir at the school like he did at the service station.

Eugene sat in the pickup truck for fifteen minutes before his mother and Lester finally emerged from the building. Inside the cabin of the truck was hot and stuffy; the heat was almost unbearable by this time. He kept his eyes on his mother, who appeared frazzled and distraught. She chatted away and made gestures at Lester. Eugene jumped out of the truck and ran towards them, startling his mother in the process.

"Eugene! What on God's good earth are you doing here?"

His mother held her chest as she spoke, such were the dramatics of Pearl Truitt.

"I left work early and thought I'd drive by the school, when I saw your car I decided to stop; I thought something may have happened to Lester."

Eugene looked at his brother as he spoke. There was no evidence of any issues that he could see, at least not right away.

"Why don't you ride with me Lester?"

Eugene ushered for his brother towards the truck. He needed time to speak to him alone.

"Yes Lester, go on over to the house with your brother; I have to meet your father somewhere. Y'all make sure you go straight home now. I don't need any other issues, please make sure to do what I say for once."

Pearl opened the driver's side door of her car and got in.

"Why you pulled me out of class, you still haven't told me."

Lester called after his mother; but she could not hear him, she already driven past them and was out of earshot.

"Come on Les we need to talk."

Eugene practically pushed his brother into the truck.

"Hey Eugene, take it easy. What's wrong with everyone? Why y'all acting so strange?"

"Shut up Lester, just shut up!"

Eugene sped out of the parking lot and unto the dirt road.

"We're going for a ride Lester; we're going to pay someone a visit." His brother had barely settled in the seat.

"Who Eugene? You heard what Momma said; we need to go straight home. Who are we going to visit, and what is all this about today? No one has answered me as yet."

Eugene did not satisfy his curiosity either; he just fixed his gaze on the road ahead. Lester noticed that they turned onto the same road they had driven the night they attacked that young girl; his stomach turned.

"Where are we going Eugene? What exactly are you planning to do here? Answer me now!"

"I know who gave information about us Lester. I am certain; could be no-one else."

Eugene kept driving; he maneuvered the truck on the rugged back road as they made their way to wherever the destination was. What did he mean by 'gave information about us'? What the hell was going on? Lester was worried and confused.

Eugene took quick breaths, his was pumped with adrenaline, and his anger built as he drove on. The boy must have seen them somehow, maybe he had followed them that night. Whatever it was; he would make that dummy confess; that was one thing that Eugene would make sure that the fool did.

Lester stayed quiet the whole time. Generally he would do whatever his brother wanted but they had gotten into enough trouble, he was not about to dig a deeper hole. He had to find a way to stop this craziness; this mysterious mission that he brother was on.

"We need to get that bastard somewhere so we can torture him and get him to admit that he was the one that started the lie about us hurting that girl."

"Who are you talking about Eugene? Did you see anyone that night?" Lester was really scared.

They drove down the road where Edna lived. Lester's heart pounded loudly in his chest; he had no idea where his brother intended to go nor did he know his plans. A car was parked in the front of Edna's place; Lester knew the house because he drop her off there on nights when she worked late in order to help their mother with her baking.

The pickup truck rolled slowly down the street; Eugene kept his head straight. He noticed the car from the service station; the man must really be that girl's father. That would explain why the car was parked in front of Edna's house. Eugene kept on driving, he was in search of another house, and he knew the one. He had seen that big dopey boy sitting with his mother on the porch many times before.

"I'm looking for that stupid boy Lester; the big dumb one who walks around alone most of the time, except when Edna's girl feels sorry and walks with him."

The mention of the girl made Lester feel empty inside. He wanted to get out of the truck and run in the direction of home.

"That's Baby Boy Eugene, he's not out to hurt anyone. Why are you looking for him?"

Lester was puzzled and confused, and got more scared as each moment went by.

Eugene explained further.

"He has to be the one who told everyone that we hurt that girl. Her daddy came by the service station today Lester; a big Black man who looks like he could toss me like an old rag doll. He said he was going to get whoever hurt his girl. Why would he be telling me that if he didn't know something?"

Eugene stopped the truck in front of the house; there was no one on the porch.

"Let's go on home Eugene; let's just go!"

Eugene refused to turn the truck around; he tapped the steering wheel with his fingers and just stared at the house.

"He must come out sometime Lester; let's just wait a few minutes."

Suddenly there was a loud bang on the back of the truck; it startled the boys and made them jump.

"What the hell are you boys looking for?" a thunderous voice sounded out.

A huge man walked up to the driver's side window. Eugene almost pissed his pants; it was the same man from earlier in the day.

"What are you doing here?"

The man banged on the truck again, and pulled at the handle of the door.

"You little shitheads have some nerve coming around here. If you are not gone by the time I count to two you will be sorry you ever drove down this street."

The whole truck shook as he pulled harder at the door. Lester yelled at his brother; he urged him to drive. Eugene fumbled with the gear; he stepped on the gas pedal, turned the steering wheel, and sped off. Lester trembled.

The man continued to yell at them.

"You mark my words; you will get what's coming to you. Don't let me catch either of you around here again or you will get whatever it is you are looking for!"

CHAPTER TWENTY-ONE

After weeks of resistance, I decided that I would not let losing *most* of my sight in one eye stop me from continuing with my life. I tried to get used to looking at things from one eye; it was difficult at first but I was determined to do it. My grandmother would prop me up on a few pillows, and help me to position whatever it was I was trying to look at; to make it easier to see. I did not want anything to be easy, I believed that there was a reason I survived what was done to me. I heard the whispers of the nurses while I was in the hospital; I saw the look on my mother's and grandmother's faces. I knew that I wouldn't be the same, and that I was in for a long period of recovery. I was determined to beat the odds; I had no other choice.

My Daddy was with me all the time, and that was the best thing that came out of this mess so far. Having him here with me was great. He made sure that I had everything I needed, and his being at my beck and call made the healing process easier. My Momma had contacted the school and made arrangements to get my assignments so that I could keep up with my studies. I decided that I was well enough to do my school work so I buried myself in my books.

Writing was the hardest of all, but in time, I found my own method and I made it work. There was much more to life; that's what Daddy always said, and I knew that my education was key to getting what I desired; it was my pathway to getting *there*. Grams preached that to me too, all the time. Telling me not to end up the way she did – stuck in Jessup. I was on a mission to make them all proud of me.

Those boys had damaged me physically, but mentally I remained strong, and grew even stronger as the days went by. Even though I was not in the classroom I was still determined to maintain good grades and stay on top of my studies. Nothing would stop me. The situation created a bump in the road of my life, and I was ready to get over it.

CHAPTER TWENTY-TWO

It had been exactly 8 weeks to the day since she opened the door and saw Baby Boy holding the beaten and bloodied body of her daughter. Since Raenelle was released from the hospital, Edna kept a close eye on her day in and out. She helped her daughter with everything - bathing, dressing, eating, and whatever else she needed done. Guilt ate away at her mind, it was sad that it took a tragedy like this to bring her this close to her only child.

When Ray left them to join the Marines, Edna went into a bit of depression. It was Grams who took to raising Raenelle, and made sure she received the emotional support that a child required. Edna sunk even deeper into her sad condition after she lost her second child. It was the final blow that took her into the abyss she thought she could never come out of. A short visit from Ray brought a glimmer of hope that she would get her life back. The joy of another pregnancy; and then to have it all *taken away* was more than she could bear.

Since this tragedy, she vowed to get herself back to the

Edna she once was, she had to do it for her daughter. She wanted to take life by *the horns* and find the strength to move on.

The courage Raenelle showed was more than Edna had expected; such resilience was unimaginable. She was her father's child without a doubt. When she spoke to her to get a sense of how she was coping, Raenelle told her that she decided not to think about the night of the rape. She boldly refused to focus on what was done to her, instead she had put all of her energy into living a normal life, and more than anything, she wanted to continue her schooling. She had worked hard to build up the courage to walk around with a patch on her eye; and she had done it without fear. This would be rather awkward for anyone to do, but it was all up to Raenelle; she said that she was ready.

Edna would watch as Raenelle adjusted the patch this way and that until she was satisfied and comfortable with its position, then painstakingly she would fix her hair into the desired style.

Edna braided her daughter's hair in small single plaits so that it would be easier for Raenelle to manage; otherwise she would wear it loose or in a bun on top of her head. On some days, Raenelle would put bows in her hair, in no particular pattern or style, and would go about her daily activities. The hair accessories made her feel pretty, she explained.

One day, out of the blue, Raenelle announced to her parents that that she was ready to return to school. She insisted that the sooner the better, and explained that she was ready for whatever was to come her way as far as going back was concerned. Although they warned of possible jeers and stares, Raenelle said that she was not worried about those things; she was alive and that was all that mattered, she added. She was determined to show the animals that tried to end her life that they did not break her. She went on to add that she had the support of her family and friends and that was good enough.

Taking into consideration all that had happened, it was only natural that Edna would refuse to go back to work for the Truitts. She had not even entertained the thought of looking for another job, that idea was placed on hold. Under the hands of the good-for-nothing boys her child had been damaged. The same boys whose snot noses she had wiped, whose tears she had tried and who she had comforted when their parents were too busy to pay them any attention. They could all go to hell for all she cared; her daughter was her priority now.

She thought about the Truitts and the fact that they were some ungrateful bastards, the entire family was that way. She really couldn't stand Pearl Truitt especially the foolishness about her social events; all that fuss just so she could impress some person or another; all for false praise. Little did she know that the same women she considered her friends spoke about her behind her back. They knew about all the women Jimmy Truitt slept around with, and all the other children he had fathered.

The *socialites* all spoke about Pearl and Jimmy and their desire to live like high class and upstanding members of society; they seemed to ignore the fact that they had produced a son who was a menace to society. They considered the Truitt boy a waste of good space on earth. He was notorious for being disrespectful – that Eugene Truitt. He was just like his father, he had no regard for other people, and possessed an attitude that portrayed him as invincible – at least in his own mind.

Edna thought of the many times Eugene would come

home and see her in the kitchen and would walk by without even saying hello. Later on he would emerge from his room and have the audacity to ask her to fix him a plate. She was tempted many times to spit in his food but knew that the good Lord above would not be pleased; she resisted the urge to yield to that temptation. Instead, she would just slap the food on the plate then pass it on to the fool; of course he never said thanks.

Now that she knew the slime had put his hands on her daughter spitting in Eugene Truitt's plate paled in comparison to what she wanted to do to him.

~~~~~~~~

Several times during the weeks after the attack on his daughter, Ray had gone to speak to the Sheriff; each time he left those meetings he got more and more frustrated. When Edna would ask what had happened, he would tell her that the Sheriff was stalling the investigation because of his close ties to Jimmy Truitt.

Ray was relentless though, he continued to spread word around town that the Truitt boys were the ones who had hurt Raenelle; he made sure everyone in their neighborhood and others in town knew what had happened. Most folks had already heard about the rape, the details of the attack were not fully released but there was chatter about it. Ray's intention was to bring awareness to the severity of the attack on his daughter. He begged and encouraged the people of the community to remain vigilant. Ray was on a mission, he further insisted that everyone be on the lookout for the boys; he asked the people of the community to band together in the name of justice.

When Percy heard about the details and who had committed the offense against his god-daughter, he insisted that they get Phillip Perkins involved. Ray knew first hand that it would be simple to get one of Phillip's associates to 'take care' of the issue and shorten the investigative and legal process. Despite the temptation, he would have none of it. This was something that he wanted to do himself.

Since Ray had found the Truitt boys lurking near Baby Boy's house, he made sure to keep an eye on the big fella and his mother. Ray even offered to take Baby Boy around to do his errands, although he knew that the young man could kill one of those boys with one blow in the right place.

He made it his business to drive around the neighborhood several times per day, just to make sure that all was well with them. At times he would sit on the porch with Baby Boy and Mrs. Johnson, with hopes that one of the fools would show his face. He was ready to hurt both of them.

Ray main desire was to be around and ready in the protective sense. Baby Boy could certainly take care of himself if pushed, but Ray didn't want the young man to get into any trouble. He was certainly not a fighter; but he was just a big Teddy Bear who loved Raenelle like a sister. Ray had other plans to avenge his daughter; plans that he knew would come to fruition soon enough; he wanted to give the authorities the chance to do the right thing. If or when sufficient time had passed, and the Sheriff had not done what was needed, Ray had already made the decision that he would have no other choice but to take matters into his own hands. This was certainly *something* he would take pleasure in doing.

CHAPTER TWENTY-THREE

Sheriff Whitefield walked around the desk and squeezed into the chair. The pressure of his belly touching the wood was uncomfortable but not painful; he only sat for a few minutes during the day, so he didn't really mind. Doc Greene warned him to change his eating habits, threatening that he wouldn't be around to keep the town in order if he ignored his health. He promised to take the Doc's advice, but he was yet to put it in practice.

The Sheriff looked at the notes he had scribbled on his pad, it was about the Porter girl. He remembered the meeting with Jimmy Truitt where they discussed the incident which involved the girl's father. He claimed that the man showed up at the Truitt house and allegedly made threats. Sheriff Whitfield listened to Truitt as he ranted and raved about his position as the warden, and his connections to this person and the other, on and on he went. Sheriff Whitfield listened, until Jimmy Truitt was satisfied that he had made his position known, he walked him out of his office; assured him that he was handling the case and thanked him for the visit.

The man was an arrogant fool. He spoke as if his position as Warden meant that he could call the shots on every arm of the law, including the Sheriff's Department.

Sheriff Whitfield knew that *he* was *the Sheriff in charge* in town, not Jimmy Truitt! Whitfield followed the law by the book; that was what he stood for, no cutting deals, greasing palms, sure he did *small favors* – but not in a case such as this. This was serious business. A child had lost her innocence in a most brutal manner, and she deserved justice regardless of who she was the part of town she came from. It did not matter who had powerful support, there would be no special treatments to hand out.

The Sheriff promptly started the investigation into the rape and beating of the young girl, and he had already gathered some evidence. The girl's father had come by several times but Whitfield was not ready to disclose any of the information he had. He did not want to encourage vigilante justice, and from the looks of that man, he would not think twice about doing something to any one of those Truitt boys.

From the first evening at the school when he questioned Lester and Eugene Truitt about the incident, Sheriff Whitfield was convinced that they knew something. The older boy seemed evasive and played it cool, but the younger Truitt boy was too nervous; fidgeting and looking everywhere else but at him. In addition to that, he waited for his brother to answer all questions; he never looked up nor answered confidently. The boy just avoided all eye contact and looked around in an uneasy manner.

When he took a drive into the woods the morning after Dr. Greene reported the incident, Sheriff Whitfield noticed tire tracks leading to a small area. Upon closer investigation he noticed that there was trampled brush and leaves with droplets of blood. He concluded that this was the area where most of the crime took place. There were also shoe prints around the small patchy section. The Sheriff found buttons, shreds of material and an empty whiskey canister. It was obvious that someone had left or forgotten to take it, obviously not caring that it would be found.

The Sheriff instructed his deputy to bag everything that could be potential evidence, while he looked around in an attempt to find anything else in the area that was potential evidence.

This area of the woods was dark, musty. There was not a single place to hide; the poor girl must have been scared for her life. There was nothing there but tall trees and sporadic areas of thick bush; the main road was a good distance away. He remembered this area of the woods from his hunting days. The Sheriff also knew that there were wild animals which roamed at night; he had seen some foxes, bears, and even snakes during his time; the area was dangerous. The young man who came to the girl's rescue was her angel for sure; she would surely have been dead by morning were it not for him.

~~~~~~~~

The Sheriff's thoughts returned to Jimmy Truitt's visit to his office. Truitt described Mr. Porter as a practical stranger who just showed up at his house and made threats. He was even angrier that the man had scared his wife and threatened his family. He described the visit as unsettling, and insisted that Sheriff Whitfield arrest the man or give him a stern warning about the repercussions of his actions. Truitt wanted a message delivered to Porter that as the Warden of the state prison, he had ties, powerful connections, and could create problems for him. The Sheriff listened, bored with the talk but gave Truitt his soapbox to make his speech.

It took almost half of an hour of his chatter before the Sheriff was able to say out loud that there was no reason to make an arrest. He explained that he needed solid evidence; an actual offense, before he could arrest any person. Truitt was not happy with his response, he said that he knew the law and wanted something done immediately. If not for the threat, he wanted something done about the lies that were being spread around town about his sons' involvement in the rape of Edna's little girl. Everyone in had heard of the incident by that time and Truitt was concerned that his boys' lives could be in danger.

Sheriff Whitfield spoke calmly to Truitt; he refused to match his antics. He assured him that the matter would be investigated and that whatever the truth was, it would be revealed in due time. He went on to assure him that if the boys had no involvement in the matter, as he – their father - believed, then there would be no need to create chaos and confusion. Truitt was still heated; the Sheriff's words meant little, it was obvious. The man announced, once again, as loudly as he could, that he was the Warden of the Georgia State Pen and anyone who dared to cross him would feel his wrath.

Whitfield was not rattled by Jimmy Truitt's words. The man was probably afraid because he knew that if his sons had committed the act they would be considered the worst of the worst. If it was proven in a court of law that Eugene and Lester were guilty, they would be put behind bars, and would not be treated too kindly.

First of all, rapist, especially those who committed the offense against children, were treated with contempt, and secondly being Jimmy Truitt's sons would double the punishment for the transgression. Sheriff Whitfield felt sorry for that whole family.

~~~~~~~~

Mrs. Truitt waited in her car in the parking lot. She was anxious to speak to her husband. When she saw him emerge from the building, she opened the car door and ran to him, her hands flayed angrily while she spoke. It looked like a one sided conversation but then he said something to her, pointed towards Sheriff Whitfield's office, got in his car, and left just her standing. Confused and embarrassed, Pearl got into her own car and drove off in the same direction as her husband.

They were quite a pair Sheriff Whitfield thought to himself; he chuckled. He watched their interaction from his office window. He walked back to his desk and sat, soon his mind drifted to that poor little girl. He imagined the torture she must have gone through on that dreaded night; again his mind went back to area in the woods where he searched.

Similarly to his conversation with Truitt, assuring him that the boys would be ok if they had not committed the crime, the Sheriff also had to assure Ray Porter that his daughter's attack would not be overlooked nor buried. He would not treat her as just *'another little black girl'* who had been attacked and left for dead. Ray had been at his office several times since the incident, he inquired about updates on the status of the case. He was adamant about the guilt of the Truitt boys and said that he wanted justice for his daughter. He boldly told the Sheriff that he knew the law and had connections with people in higher positions than Jimmy Truitt. It was obvious that he too was aware of the Warden's arrogance and would have no problem bringing the man down to size.

Whitfield admired Ray Porter's fearlessness; he was a confident man, one who spoke only words which he meant, no idle words came from his lips. With that attitude, size and built the man clearly was a force to be reckoned with. The fact of the matter was that a girl was raped and beaten so severely that she lost sight in one eye; someone had to pay for it. Justice had to be served.

~~~~~~~~

The following day, Sheriff Whitfield headed to Dalton Johnson's house to speak to the young man. Baby Boy, as he was better known, had spoken to a deputy, but he had refused to say what he had seen on the night in question. Even though the officer assured Baby Boy that he was in no trouble and that his account of the incident would actually help to bring the person or persons who hurt Raenelle to justice; the young man still refused. He reason was that Raenelle didn't die and that was all that mattered – he didn't want to start any problems with people. Those were his words, according to the deputy's report.

Sheriff Whitfield decided that he would just talk to the boy and try to get him to open up about what he saw; he had to get this case moving.

Whitfield pulled up in front of the Johnsons' house; he noticed three people sitting on the porch. The sound of the tires running over loose gravel made them all look up and into the direction of the short drive way. Sheriff Whitfield recognized Ray Porter; he was the first to stand up, followed by Baby Boy.

"Good evening folks." Sheriff Whitfield said as he walked towards the porch. He rested one foot on the first step then put his elbow on his knee for leverage; he took off his hat and nodded to Mrs. Johnson who sat with her Bible clutched in her hands. She didn't seem to notice him.

"Mr. Porter, we meet again."

Ray nodded and Baby Boy did the same.

"Dalton, how are you doing son?"

A warm summer breeze picked up and leaves danced around in circles; after the dust settled and the leaves stopped dancing, Sheriff Whitfield climbed the few steps to the porch and continued to speak.

"I have a few things to speak to you about Dalton. I need to get a good understanding about what you saw *that night.* You just need to tell me what you saw and where you found Miss Raenelle. That's all son."

Baby Boy looked nervously at Ray; he received a nod of approval and indicated by shaking his head that he was ready to answer the Sheriff's questions.

"Now you said that you saw the Truitt boys earlier that night is that right Dalton?"

"Yes Sir, that's right Sir."

Baby Boy twisted his hands nervously.

"Can you tell me exactly where they were and what you remember seeing them do?"

The Sheriff pulled out a little pad and started to write. Baby Boy gave the Sheriff the same account that he had given to Ray and Edna; the story of how the boys followed Raenelle in their pickup truck. He told the Sheriff how they dragged Raenelle and pushed her inside the vehicle before driving off. When asked why he didn't try to stop them, Baby Boy said that he didn't want to mess with Jimmy Truitt's boys. The Sheriff repeated questions in different forms but Baby Boy stuck to his answers; there could be no denying that he had told the truth and that what he was said was what he remembered seeing and hearing on the night in question.

After he questioned Baby Boy and was satisfied that he had gotten enough information, the Sheriff decided to ask Ray the inevitable.

"Mr. Porter when can we speak to Raenelle?"

The sudden silence was deafening. Ray shifted in his seat.

"My daughter is not ready for that yet Sir, she just wants to continue on with school and her normal activities. Please give her a chance to settle."

Ray stood up, he seemed to grow taller, Whitfield swallowed hard.

"I understand Mr. Porter but we do need to get her account of what happened that night; as painful as it may be, she needs to tell her side. We need to collaborate Dalton's story if this investigation is to progress."

Ray just stared at the man, he knew what he had said saying was true, but the thought of having his daughter relive those horrible moments was too much for him to bear. She was doing just fine and he couldn't risk anything that may send her back into depression.

"I will get back to you as soon as I can Sheriff; I have to prepare her, she needs to be ready to talk about it; and it will be entirely up to her. I won't push her."

The Sheriff asked to be notified of when the interview could take place. He reminded Ray of the time constraints, then thanked the men for their time. He tipped his hat and bade the group goodbye.

"Mr. Ray."

Baby Boy cut the silence that filled the air. Ray turned to face the young man and waited for him to speak.

"Do you think Raenelle can talk about what happened? I seen what they did Mr. Ray, she shouldn't have to repeat none of that; that's just not right."

Ray said nothing, he knew that the interview with Raenelle and the Sheriff would be something that could not be avoided. Since he sought justice through the right channels, he had to follow through with what was required. He would speak with Edna and Raenelle later on; it would be up to his daughter to decide if she could handle repeating what happened to her that night.

"It will all work out Son, don't you worry about it. It will all work out."

Ray made sure that Baby Boy and his mother were settled in, and then walked to Edna's and Ida May's house. Raenelle would be waiting for him.

CHAPTER TWENTY-FOUR

It had been difficult to return to school; everyone stared at me all the time, I heard from my friend Ruth that people were saying *things*. I didn't care much; whatever they said did not make me who the person I was, and none of them were friends of mine anyway. I was prepared to tell off anyone of them who dared come to me and tried to speak mess about me. Prior to the incident, there were only a few people I actually had conversations with at school anyway; so it really didn't matter.

When I returned to Jessup High, Ruth would walk with me in the hallways and sit with me at lunch. I had lived through my horrible ordeal therefore a few snickers and stares from idiots at school, were nothing in comparison. Strangely enough, the patch made me feel strong - invincible. In a way I felt like a tough girl. At first, I was not sure how I would handle reading, swimming, or some of my other usual activities knowing that I had this *thing* covering my eye. In time though it became just a *thing* on my face. The fools who hurt me had done so with the intention of leaving me for dead, and even though I survived, I'm sure they thought that I would be ashamed to show myself. I was happy to be alive and able to carry on with my life even if I looked different. There was definitely a change in me; I really felt renewed, like something divine had transformed me.

Many thought it would be hard for me to be in the same building with one of the people responsible for my disfigurement. Momma was especially nervous about that but I assured her that I would be just fine. I just avoided the idiot Truitt boy at all cost. I would see when his mother dropped him off in her fancy car – that woman who was so fake.

He still played football and was hailed a hero for the 'incredible' pass that helped to win the championship; that meant nothing to me, he was dead to me. In my heart I knew that my Daddy was going to find a way to make them pay and if needed, I would help him; I did not know how or when but I just knew it would happen. That was my comfort. They were scum, I would spit on them if I had the chance, but then again, that would be a waste of good saliva.

~~~~~~~~

"Come on Raenelle, it's time for recess."

The bell indicating break time had rung but I had not noticed, I was deep in thought.

"Ok Ruthie, I'm coming."

I packed away the books that were laid out on my desk and followed my friend outside. Summer was about to come to an end but the sun was still bright in the sky, its rays would be welcomed once I got outside. I would much rather be here at school, feeling the sunshine on my skin, than laying up in some hospital bed or shut in at home.

Ruth and I made our way outside and immediately I noticed him, he stood across the yard, that criminal Lester Truitt. I froze; Ruth noticed.

"Come on Rae, let's go to the other side."

She grabbed my arm but I pulled away. An unknown force steered me towards him. I walked without fear, but I felt like I had no control over my own legs. It was as if someone else had taken over my body. Lester looked over and noticed that I was walking in his direction. The boys who were with him stood still, I could hear Ruth's steps behind me, she was almost running. She whispered my name, she begged me to stop. Lester put his hands in his pockets as I neared him. He looked nervous as if he was not sure what to do. His eyes darted from me to the boys and back to me. I kept walking and stopped only when I was inches from him. The boys around him started to snicker; that fueled the rage that had risen in me.

"Take a look at me."

I pointed my finger to his face; he looked at me with gloomy, weak eyes. He didn't move a single bit; he seemed paralyzed. I continued to speak.

"You and your dumb ass brother thought I was dead didn't you? You took turns and you little shits stuck your stink little willies in me, spat, and pissed on me, then left me to die. Remember that asshole?"

I was in a frenzied state. The snickers turned into giggles but I did not stop, the fire inside me grew.

"Let me tell you this, you little boy that follows every order that your brother gives, you puppet who jumps every time he tells you to. You are going to be sorry you ever laid your nasty ass hands on this girl. Yea that's right, look away now you fool, but be prepared because my Daddy will make sure you feel the same pain I did. Believe me, you will wish that you were dead before that happens because it will be 100 times worse than what I felt. Close your eyes and remember that night, you will live to regret that you had ever did this to me Lester Punk Weasel Truitt!"

When I said his name he just stared at me, he looked dazed and confused. When I was done speaking, I spat at his feet, adjusted the patch on my eye then turned and started to walk away. I stopped in my tracks and went back to where he remained standing. I was not done! He was still there; he hung his head in shame. I said my last piece.

"And one more thing, you can tell your puppet master brother Eugene to watch his back because Ray Porter will be coming after him too. You make sure to tell him that."

I spat again; flipped my braids and then walked away.

Ruth grabbed my arm and walked with me; she led me away from the crowd that had gathered. When we were out of earshot, she turned to me.

"Stink little willies, really Rae?"

I couldn't help but smile. It was the first time I spoke out loud about that night and I guess she was as surprised as everyone else was. Ruth had never questioned me about it before and I'm not sure if I would have wanted to speak about it even if she did. Today was different, I didn't care who heard. I felt free.

We found some shade under one of the trees in the schoolyard and leaned against the trunk. I took a deep breath and looked over to where I had left Lester standing; He was no longer amongst the crowd; some of them had walked away, he included. Those who remained were making hand gestures, pointing to where I was, and some were even laughing. I wasn't bothered by any of it.

"I said what I had to say Ruth and I meant every word of it. I just wish his stupid brother was around to hear me as well; I hate them both and they will pay! That much I know!"

That afternoon, Daddy picked me up from school, just as he had been doing during the weeks since I had returned there. Normally he would be chatting up a storm; his way of cheering me up. That day I didn't need *spirit lifting* but I figured that if he tried, I would go along with it anyway.

He was unusually quiet on the ride home, but I didn't think much of it. I assumed that he didn't feel much like talking. I was ok with that because I felt like a weight was lifted from off my shoulders after I had let Lester know how I felt about him and his brother. I looked out the window as we drove on and watched the heat rise from the street when we stopped at the traffic light in town. It was a really hot day, sweat beaded on my forehead. The air condition in the car did not seem to help. We continued to drive on in silence for a while.

"Rae, Baby Girl."

My daddy's baritone voice broke the silence.

I turned to look at him; he kept his eyes on the road but continued to speak.

"Sheriff Whitfield wants to talk to you about what happened. How do you feel about that?"

I knew that that request would come at some point. Before today, I would have refused, but the confidence I had acquired spoke *for* me. I believed I was ready to meet with

Sheriff Whitfield. I had nothing more to be ashamed of.

"Sure Daddy, I have no problem doing that."

He quickly glanced at me. There was a look of absolute surprise on his face. I guess my response was not what he had expected. He spoke again.

"Don't worry Princess, I will be right there with you."

I looked at him and smiled. I was not afraid of those Truitt fools anymore, they couldn't hurt me. My Daddy was there to protect me.

When we arrived at the house, Grams had already taken up her usual position on the porch; as any other day, a bowl of string beans sat on her lap. She snapped the heads off almost with a precise rhythm; the snap was in unison with her humming. It was an activity that Grams said relaxed her. I could hear her as I got out of the car.

Momma came to the front door when she heard the car drive up. Since the incident she was so attentive that I sometimes felt stifled. I didn't complain though, I let her have her time; guilt was probably tearing her apart. I wished she didn't feel that way. It was not her but those monsters who caused me the pain and anguish that I suffered. Besides, it was not the first time that I had gone to the store to get things on my own. Then the thought came to me, I couldn't remember the last time that I saw Momma smoke a cigarette. I walked up the steps, went over to Grams and kissed her on the cheek; she smiled and continued on with her snapping.

"How was school today Rae?"

She looked much older now, there were worry lines across her ginger complexioned forehead.

"I had a good day Grams."

I did not mention anything about my confrontation with Lester Truitt, it was not necessary, she would only worry more. Daddy had placed my school bag and some books on one of the chairs in the porch; he waved to Grams and Momma as he walked back down the steps.

"I'm going to check on Baby Boy and his mother."

Just mere seconds after Daddy had started out of the yard there was a loud explosion. The place shook with a force I had never felt. Grams' bowl of peas flew from her lap. Smoke and flames bellowed from the direction of Baby Boy's house; Daddy ran towards the blaze, so did my mother and grandmother, as screams followed. I stood frozen on the porch; my bag fell with a loud thud; I had just picked it up from where Daddy had rested it. The blaze grew higher and I saw black smoke in the direction where my parents and grandmother had gone.

My Daddy finally emerged through the grey curtain, he held Baby Boy's mother in his arms, and her body was limp. Daddy put her on the ground and stated to perform CPR; I ran down to where she lay; it was a terrible scene and I couldn't hold back my tears.

"Daddy, Daddy, what happened to Mrs. Johnson? Is she ok Daddy?"

He continued to compress her chest and breathe into her mouth. She remained motionless. Momma, Grams and Baby Boy arrived soon after. Baby Boy had an arm over my mother's shoulder and one over Grams. His clothes and hair were covered with soot. I looked at Daddy, as he tried hard to revive Mrs. Johnson. My mother dropped to her knees, leaving Grams to bear the weight of Baby Boy. Mrs. Johnson took a deep breath after some minutes then coughed. Daddy helped her to a sitting position, told her to take some more breaths then announced that he was taking her to the hospital.

Sirens could be heard coming from the town; the house was still on fire. When Daddy got Mrs. Johnson to the car, Baby Boy ran towards it and sat in the back with his mother. He had stood and watched and he hugged himself the entire time my Daddy was tried to help Mrs. Johnson. He didn't want to be separated from her, he forgot about himself, he wanted to make sure that his mother would be ok. Mama and Grams decided to stay and wait for the fire truck to arrive. Other neighbors had gathered and I stood in the middle of the street a bit dazed; they were not sure what to do. I watched as Daddy drove off at full speed.

"Mama what happened? How did the house get caught on fire?"

Momma just shook her head as did Grams. My heart raced as fast as the blaze, thank goodness there was no threat to other houses around. The fire truck finally arrived, followed closely by Sheriff Whitfield and two of his deputies. The firemen worked quickly and vigorously to put out the blaze, as the crowd of onlookers continued to grow. Neighbors were relieved to know that Mrs. Johnson would be ok but still curious to know what caused the fire. No one had any answers.

CHAPTER TWENTY-FIVE

Eugene hid the gas can in the back area of the service station garage. He felt he had to put it away on the back shelves so that it would be out of sight. There was really no reason to hide it because a gas can at a service station was no strange thing. His arm burned where his shirt had caught on fire and the material had stuck to his skin. Damn! It was very painful. He was a little careless but he had done the job he set out to do. His message was clear! He did not let Lester know what he had planned; his little brother had turned into a little wimpy pussy lately. He would have tried to stop him from doing what he had done. Eugene was determined to send *his* message *loud* and clear; and that he did. The painful grimace on his face turned into a satisfied grin.

Earlier in the day Lester had the nerve to tell him that the little bitch had embarrassed him in front of everyone at school. Eugene had gone to pick up his brother and that was when he recounted the story. What an idiot he was, he was punked by a little one-eyed bitch. He was ashamed of his him, that stupid Lester! If that were him, she would be still on the school grounds looking for her other fucking eye; that was for sure! That would be the price he would make her pay, especially since she dared to talk about the size of their penises in front of their friends. Who did that busted little bitch think she was?

Since the incident, Eugene had devised many plans in his head to finish off the girl, but he turned his vengeful attention to the big dummy – Baby Boy. He was sure that the fool had seen them that night; people were talking around town.

Baby Boy was big and intimidating, and could easily snap his neck but Eugene was still determined to handle his business. He was Jimmy Truitt's son; he was capable of finding ways of putting fear into anyone at will; that was a fact.

Early in the day, Eugene had snuck under Baby Boy's house and poured gasoline on a stack of old boarded beams there. He waited for Ray Porter to leave to pick up *the girl* from school; he timed it perfectly. He also had a mixture in a bottle that would create a fantastic explosion. He was sure that his plan would work. Burn that old bitch ass house down; blow it to pieces and show that fucker that he needed to shut his dumb ass mouth. Did he not know that the Truitts never sat and waited for things to happen? Stupid retarded boy!

~~~~~~~~

Baby Boy sat on the porch oblivious to the world around him, he and his momma sat staring at nothing in particular. Ray had gone to pick up Raenelle and drove out on schedule; Eugene felt around in his pocket for the box of matches that he planned to use to light the piece of cloth he had brought. Shit! He had forgotten them the damned matched. Shit, shit! He had to hurry back to the service station before Ray Porter returned; he could not risk getting caught.

Sweat ran down his face and from his arm pits as he hustled across the field and onto the dirt road that led to the station. He looked back several times to make sure that no one saw him. His fingers trembled as he raced to the back of the building and retrieved the box of matches; they were right where he left them. He hurriedly grabbed them and placed them in his pockets, he was still wearing his mechanic's overalls. He wanted to make it back to Baby Boy's house before Ray returned. His forgetfulness had cost him some time.

Eugene sprinted back to the dumb boy's house. It seemed longer to get there this time around than it did initially, but he made it back just in the nick of time. Ray Porter's car was not in sight, and that was a good thing.

Eugene crept back under the house and peeked through the crack of the porch to see if the boy and his mother were still sitting there. He heard voices inside; it was the boy, he was asking his mother if she was ready for supper. Shit! They could get trapped inside and they could die, Eugene felt his throat closing as his heart pounded. He thought for a few seconds, his breathing was shallow; the smell of damp dirt filled his nostrils. He didn't want to kill them but he was already there and he had to finish what he started.

"Fuck it! It's too late now, I'm going to burn this shit down."

He crawled out from under the house and knelt at the side, careful to remain out of view from anyone who might walk past. He took the matches from his pockets and lit the gas soaked rag that hung from the bottle that contained the flammable mixture. The blaze caught him off guard, and in a panic he shook the bottle, the sleeve of his overall stated to burn, he dropped the bottle, kicked it under the house and ran.

He stopped for a minute to catch his breath all the while slapping his sleeve to extinguish the flames. When he was satisfied that the sleeve was no longer burning, he continued to run towards the station, and a few minutes after, when he was halfway through the big field, he heard a loud boom followed by screams; he turned to see black smoke and flames rising from the house. His adrenaline soared and he laughed uncontrollably, from nervousness mostly, but also from a sinister feeling of triumph.

Screw them all! Didn't they know that he was Eugene Truitt? He felt larger than life. Let them watch that stupid fool and his nutcase of a mother burn. In the end, Eugene thought, it would be worth the horrible stinging sensation he felt on his arm.

When he got back to the gas station Eugene carefully removed his overalls; some of its rough material had gotten stuck to his skin. He looked around for a first aid kit, he knew that there had to be one somewhere. He found the old rusty box and opened it; he was sure that it had to have been there for decades, the bandage fell apart in his hand and the cream smelled rancid. He threw the entire thing to the ground. He found a container of petroleum jelly and for a second wondered why it was there; he brushed away the thought and then applied some of the gooey substance to the area. There were fluid filled bubbles where he got burned. He gritted his teeth from the pain; he pulled on his regular shirt, made sure that the building was properly secured, and then drove home. He would have to wait until he got to his house to put medication on the burn.

CHAPTER TWENTY-SIX

Ray waited anxiously at the hospital to get an update on Baby Boy and Mrs. Johnson; an emergency room physician finally came out and assured him that the pair was doing well. He further explained that they had both suffered from smoke inhalation and needed oxygen, but other than that they would be just fine. An overnight stay for observation was all that was required, and if all went well they would be released the next day. Ray was happy to hear the news, he had a flash back of the blast and remembered his fear that they had lost Mrs. Johnson.

He was allowed to see Baby Boy, who was alert; Ray spoke briefly to the young man, assured him that everything was fine with his mother and himself, and promised him that he would return the next morning. Ray explained that he needed to rush back home to make sure that his family was doing ok. He peeked in on Mrs. Johnson on his way out; she slept peacefully; the oxygen mask was securely fastened over her nose and mouth.

When he arrived at the house, he notice that there were several people still lingering on the street. The fire had already been put out and only the charred remains of what was once the Johnson's home remained.

The family had lost everything. He noticed Edna had waited outside for him; she walked up to the car, waited for him to step out, and then hugged him. It was as if she needed reassurance that what happened earlier would not happen to them as well. Ray held her close. He kissed her on the forehead and whispered softly to her.

"I'm here Edna. Are you ok?"

He squeezed her arm, she shook her head '*yes*'.

"How are they Ray? Is Mrs. Johnson ok?"

Ray repeated what he was told by the doctors, and then asked about Raenelle and Grams.

"They are in the house" Edna replied. "Raenelle is very worried."

Ray went into the house and headed straight to the room that Raenelle shared with her grandmother. Grams held her granddaughter close; they both rocked back and forth in silence.

"It's ok Princess, they both will be just fine." Ray announced.

When she heard her father's voice and the good news about her neighbors, Raenelle jumped up and fell into his arms; she sobbed.

"Why Daddy, why did their house burn?" She asked.

"I don't know baby girl, but we will get to the bottom of it. The good thing is that no life was lost. Don't worry, everything is going to be alright." Ray comforted his child.

Her sobbing subsided. After he was sure that his family was safe Ray decided to check the charred remains of the Johnson's home. He thought about the questions he would have for Sheriff Whitfield. He needed to find the man as soon as possible. Certain events were all too coincidental; first the Truitt boys drove past the house, and now it caught fire and burned to the ground? No, something seemed fishy, those boys were involved somehow; he felt it.

Luckily, the Sheriff's car was still at the Johnson's property; Ray looked around the area for a bit and then searched among the men, he spotted Whitfield and walked over to him.

"May I have a word with you?" He gestured to the Sheriff to join him a little way from the other men.

Whitfield handed something to one of his deputies and motioned to Ray that he would join him in the clearing. No one would be able to hear their conversation there.

"What's on your mind Mr. Porter?"

The Sheriff adjusted his suspenders.

"Do you have any idea what happened here?"

Ray waited for Whitfield to answer. He had used his is own investigative skills and had an idea of the fire came about but was not ready to reveal what he knew; he would wait for the perfect moment.

"We're not one hundred percent sure, but it looks like arson. That's our preliminary finding; there were traces of an accelerant found in the rubble".

Ray nodded, just as he'd suspected. He chatted a bit more with the Sheriff, he mentioned that the request to speak with Raenelle would be granted, especially in light of the events that happened that day. The Sheriff accepted, confirmed that he would speak with the girl as soon as he could, and then shook hands with Ray. The men departed, Ray went back to his family and Whitfield continued to direct the investigation. Ray was more than ready to put things into motion. It was time for action!

CHAPTER TWENTY-SEVEN

Eugene crept into the house. He used the side door closest to the kitchen as his point of entrance. He wanted to avoid his parents at all cost, at least until he could clean himself up and bandage his burnt arm. He already had a story to tell them if they saw his arm and asked questions. He would say that it happened at work, a radiator accident or something.

The kitchen was dark by this time, all of the lights were turned off and only a small dimly-lit lamp remained on in the hallway. That was good enough for him, the lamp produced just enough light for him to find his way around. He took off his boots, placed them in the shoe box next to the door then tipped-toed towards his room. He heard his parent's voice coming from the living room area. They were commenting on a radio broadcast, his father's voice bellowed above his mother's. When Eugene got to his room, Lester was seated on his bed.

"What the hell are you doing in here Lester? Get out my damn room!"

He was startled more than anything else.

Lester noticed the rag wrapped around his brother's arm.

"What happened to your arm?"

Lester got up from the bed and walked towards his brother. Eugene stepped back and shut the door.

"Mind your damn business Lester; I said get out of my room!"

Lester reached for Eugene's arm.

"What happened to your arm Eugene?"

"I hurt it at work, a radiator cover flew off and the steam burned me. Are you satisfied now?"

"Why didn't you just say so then? What's with all the anger and hiding? Are you telling the truth Eugene?"

Lester breathed heavily and his anger grew. He had heard about the fire across town. He knew the house; it was where that boy lived, the one who Eugene was looking for; they had driven past it the other day. His brother's suspicious actions made him suspect that something was wrong.

"What the hell do you mean if I'm telling the truth? What are you saying Lester? I said I burned my arm on a damn radiator. Now get the hell out of my room! I'm telling you that for the last time."

Eugene opened the door and pointed for his brother to leave. Lester walked past him, he stared his brother in the eyes and shook his head as he made his way out. He knew that his brother was lying, he could feel it.

After Lester left, Eugene took the cloth from his arm;

the pain was excruciating; since there was nothing at the station that he could use to soothe it, it was important for him to do so as soon as possible. Now that he was at home, he needed to find something; they had *burn cream* in the house somewhere, he was sure of that.

He took off the rest of his clothes and headed to the bathroom; he stopped in the hallway. Lester was blabbing to his parents about the fire, telling them that there was nothing left of the house. His father blew it off as a careless accident, he said that he had heard about it from one of his officers. He was not the least bit concerned. His mother, on the other hand, asked about the fate of the people who lived there. Lester told her that he didn't know and soon after his mother changed the subject.

She never asked about Edna and her family, even though she knew that they lived in the same area where the fire occurred. Eugene went into the bathroom and did his best to take care of his arm; the thing did not look good at all. He thought about his brother and his recent change of attitude; Lester had become a real disappointment, the stupid fool. It was impossible for Eugene to trust him. He was sure that if they put pressure on him and asked him hard questions about *that night* that he would crumble and sell them out.

Eugene did not like scene that played out in his head.

~~~~~~~~

Later on that evening, Lester lay on his bed; he stared at the ceiling. Images of the rape and *torture* filled his head; as they did every night. The screams and sobs from Edna's girl followed him every day. It affected him in many ways; his performance on the football field had dropped significantly. He messed up plays, missed wide open throws and got sacked more times that he could count.

Ever since the winning throw to capture the title, it had all gone downhill. The coach threatened to take away his position if Lester didn't improve his game. In addition to all that, the girl had walked up to him in the school-yard and embarrassed him, patch over her eye and all. That made him feel even more like a monster. He allowed Eugene to manipulate him into doing something that he knew was wrong and he had suffered ever since.

The girl had walked up to him with so much confidence. It was as if she had no fear, and the words that came out of her mouth shrank him to the lowest level he had ever been in his life. He deserved it all, he concluded; she had all rights to spit on him, what he and his brother did to her was horrible; unforgivable. The consequences for such a crime was not something he was prepared to pay despite it all. There had to be another way.

The fire at Baby Boy's house, Eugene with a burnt arm; Lester knew that there was a connection somewhere. His brother did want to harm that boy, he had said so. He would try to get some sleep, but vowed to figure out what he would do on the next day. He would have no more of Eugene's crap, it was time he made his own decisions. He refused to be bullied or forced to do things that he well knew were wrong. No more messing up and guilt trips. This had gone far enough.

~~~~~~~~

The next morning, Lester woke up and quickly got ready for school. His night was restless, he hardly slept. The smell of bacon wafted in the air but unlike other mornings when he would rush downstairs to eat, he took his time. He wasn't really hungry, he just wanted to get dressed and leave, mostly because he wanted to avoid his brother.

He picked up his books and made his way down to the kitchen with the intention to leave through the back door. When he entered the kitchen, his mother was already seated at the small table sipping coffee. Mahalia had finished the eggs and grits, and had already set a place for him and his brother. Rather than suffer through a barrage of questions from his mother about his skipping his meal, Lester decided to sit down.

"Good morning Son, nice day today, huh?"

His mother said those words as if she and he had the best and closest relationship in the world.

He played along.

"Good morning Mother."

Lester took small bites of the food as he forced himself to eat half of the portion on the plate. Nothing had taste; he just went through the motions. His mother sipped her coffee and stared out the window.

"Oh by the way, Eugene left early this morning, I could take you to school or you could walk, it's your choice."

Not having his brother around made Lester relax a bit. He was in no mood to ride with Eugene, but he was curious to know why he had left so early.

His curiosity peaked and he asked his mother if she knew the reason behind the early departure.

"He said something about a car coming in early for service" his mother responded nonchalantly.

Lester had his suspicions; the reason given was nonsense. Eugene never went to work early, appointment or not. The owner of the service station owed their father for shortening a jail sentence for one of his sons, hence the reason that Eugene still had a job.

"By the way Lester, the Sheriff is coming by this evening, he wants to talk to every member of the family. It's about Edna's girl again. I just want that whole thing to be behind us once and for all. I know you boys had nothing to do with it, so we will put all of that to rest today. Edna will know the truth and perhaps return to work, I miss her so. She made everything here sparkle, hmm."

Pearl stared off into space when she spoke. Mahalia shifted from one foot to the next and continued to do the dishes.

Lester's heart drummed loudly, the Sheriff planned to come by to question them? What would he say? He hid his fear and panic from his mother. In her usual fashion, she paid no attention to him anyway, she had returned to her appointment book and busied herself by flipping through the pages. He pushed the plate away.

"I'm leaving now Mother.

He kissed her on the cheek.

"Have a good day at school" she called after him.

He was through the door before the words left her lips.

~~~~~~~~

Lester hurried down the dusty road, the air was humid for that time of day. Several cars passed by, whipping up dust and debris; he stopped a few times and turned his back to avoid any of it from hitting him in the face. He didn't want to be in school that day, he doubted that he would be able to concentrate; there were pressing issues on his mind. He increased his pace as he neared the school, thankful that none of the cars that passed was that girl's father. Eugene had described him as a big man and Lester thought that he had exaggerated but when he gave them the scare that night in front of Baby Boy's house, Lester knew that he would piss his pants if he had an encounter with him. The man was huge. He knew that he would not be able to handle a one-on-one with that man.

The school yard came into full view, several other students milled about, others stood in groups, engaged in chatter. Lester searched among them for his clique and spotted them under the same tree where the girl had said all those things about him and Eugene, then spat at him. He took a breath and walked in their direction. He hoped that no one would bring up the incident, but if they did he planned to laugh it off.

"Did you hear about the fire across town last evening?"

That was the first question that greeted him. It was from Fenton, a kid who could catch a ball thrown from any angle. Lester shrugged his shoulders, not showing much interest.

Fenton continued.

"Yeah, I heard the house burned flat, and they think someone did it on purpose."

The other boys chimed in, all providing additional information and varying interpretations of the news. Some said that the big boy burned his house on purpose to kill his own mother, while others said that it was because of a quarrel with another neighbor. Lester new differently but kept it to himself; his brother's bandaged arm came to mind. He stood expressionless as the rest of the boys continued to discuss the fire.

The bell rang to his great relief, and they all filed into their respective class lines to go into the building; none of them mentioned the incident with the girl. It was then that he saw him, the huge man walking his daughter into the building. Lester was able to get a better look at the man's size and built. He was even more intimidating in the daylight. The girl shot a glance in his direction, she held her gaze for a few minutes and for that short time, Lester felt the same hate and contempt she spewed at him the day before. The man kept walking, he held his head high, squared his shoulders, and strides were confident as he held his daughter's hand and escorted her. Beads of perspiration began to form across Lester's forehead, his hand trembled.

"Are you okay there man?"

Fenton nudged him; he had stopped dead in his tracks and didn't even realize it.

"Yeah, yeah." He replied nervously. *'What if the man turned to see him standing there? What if he came after him?'* he thought.

He willed his feet to walk and continued along with his classmates. Maybe he should fake a stomach ache and ask to go home, but he soon changed his mind for fear that he may run into the man, he dared not take the chance. Besides all that, there was the Sheriff's visit later on, he had to think about what to say. It was better to stay in school, he thought; he would be safe there for the time being.

Eugene sat in his pickup truck, he had parked outside of the service station. He was still unsettled about Lester's questions, the fire, and the stupid burn on his arm. The thing looked worse this morning than it did last evening. It had multiple fluid filled bubbles here and there and had turned a weird shade of green and purple combined. In addition to all that was going on, his mother had announced to him that morning that the Sheriff would be paying them a visit. He wanted to ask them questions about the rape and beating of Edna's girl, she had explained. Prior to last night, Eugene would have had no reason to doubt that his brother would have his back but the little punk made it obvious that he would crack if enough pressure was put on him.

The late summer heat made the inside of the pickup feel like an oven; it made no difference to him at the moment though, his mind was on all the problems that he had. It would all be fine if he could get his brother to stick to their claim of not having anything to do with the rape and beating; if need be, they could vouch for each other. He wondered if he should try to talk to Lester; maybe there he still time. He would remind him about their promised to take care of each other no matter what. Maybe that was the answer.

He looked into the station; the sickly kid slowly packed merchandise on the shelves, oblivious to anyone or anything else around. Instead of parking in the back and going into the mechanics area as he should, Eugene turned on the engine and drove towards the school; he had to speak with his brother. He had to devise a plan with him.

Their stories needed to be collaborated so that there would be no doubt when the Sheriff questioned them. The fact that their parents would be present made the impending visit even more dreadful. Their mother's presence was not such a big deal, she was so certain that her boys were *good*; so certain that they would never get into any trouble – no matter what was said; she would stand firm with that belief. Their father, on the other hand, was totally different in his way of thinking. His concern would be about saving his name and position as Warden. That was all that mattered to him, perhaps if he had taken the time to do things with them, and had become involved in their extracurricular activities, then they may have not have been so easily led to engage in foolish things.

Eugene got to the school and parked the truck at the side of the road, he decided that he would sit and wait until the morning break, then go into the school yard and get his brother. He rolled down the window and turned on the radio. He touched the dial and found a country music station. A man sang about *losing his lady love to another man;* he crooned about his regrets – *he forgot to pay attention to her and forgot to pay the bills, but in the end he was happy because he still had his truck.*

Eugene laughed, and thought the story was a shame! Those songs were all the same Eugene thought to himself, but he hummed along with the tune anyway. He took another look at his arm, it hurt really badly; he should have had it checked out by a doctor or nurse. He thought that it looked infected. After his talk with Lester, the clinic would be his next stop. If they asked questions, he would tell them that he burned it on a radiator, much like the story he planned to tell his parents and what he told Lester. The sudden thump on the window startled Eugene, he jerked forward, banging his injured arm on the steering wheel.

"Fuck, fuck!" Pain shot through his body.

He looked in the rearview mirror and instantly recognized the car, it belonged to Ray Porter. Eugene fumbled with the keys in the ignition, he tried to start the pickup but the vehicle refused to budge. He forgot about the pain in his arm, he tried to put the truck into gear but nothing happened, he then tried again. Still nothing!

Ray walked angrily to the driver's side window; he

banged on it too, all the while yelling at Eugene to step out of the car. Eugene continued his attempt to get the truck started.

"Are you here to take her from school? Are you here to finish her off? Why the hell are you lurking in the shadows of these trees outside the school yard? What are you doing here? Answer me, boy!"

The struggle with the ignition continued; Eugene's hands shook uncontrollably.

"I don't want your daughter, she ain't all that. He spat."

The doors were locked and the window up. Eugene felt that he could speak freely. There was no way this man would dare to break his window.

The snide comment from Eugene added fuel to the fire. A baseball bat appeared, and with one powerful blow, glass shattered.

"What did you just say? You cowardly bastard! Did you just say something about my daughter?"

With a force like nothing he had ever felt before, Eugene felt Ray grab him by his shirt collar and pull with all his might. The pressure from the rough material pressing against his throat cut Eugene's air supply, he could hardly breathe. He kicked his feet wildly but the man only pulled tighter on his shirt. His burnt arm rubbed hard against the seat of the pickup truck. He wasn't sure which hurt worst, his neck being squeezed by the pressure being applied or raw flesh burning fiercely because of the friction. The man showed no signs of letting up.

Eugene gasped for air, his breathing became shallow, and just as he was about to sink into darkness, he found that he to breathe again. His lungs filled with air once again; he coughed. Ray had let go of his chokehold; but he had stuck his head into the cabin of the truck and had gotten as close as he could to Eugene's face.

"Stay the fuck away from my daughter, from my family and from Baby Boy. The next time I catch your sorry ass on my street you will not live to tell about it. You can deliver that message to your father as well, you son-of-a-bitch."

He looked into Eugene's beady blue eyes. The boy was scared. Ray was sure that he had soiled himself.

"The next time you may not be this lucky. You hear me! That is not a game nor a threat boy. IT IS A PROMISE! Now get the hell away from here. You can run to your Daddy. Tell him I, Ray Porter, smashed your truck. Tell him he can come on because I got something for him too! And one last thing boy. You and your cowardly brother will pay for hurting my daughter, and you will also pay for burning Mrs. Johnson's house. Believe that!"

Eugene shook with fear. He felt something warm running down his legs, the strong smell of urine filled his nostrils. He had pissed himself; the yellow liquid settled into his shoes.

~~~~~~~~

Ray started to walk back to his car and turned to look at the truck as the engine started. A very scared Eugene Truitt made a U-turn and sped off at top speed past his parked car.

The sight of that truck parked outside his daughter's school had awaken the beast inside of him; he could have easily killed that boy. The thought that his baby had to face the other monster inside those school walls every day was torture enough. There was no need to have one lurk on the outside as well.

There was no doubt in Ray's mind that he had scared the hell out of the sociopathic Truitt weasel; the idiot had the audacity to lurk outside the school yard. There was no reason why he should be parked outside of the school where the girl he had raped and tortured attended. He did not try to hide, instead he sat in his truck as if he felt invincible, untouchable, and covered with some protective armor. Ray knew that the little punk had probably gone running to his daddy. Ray welcomed a one-on-one confrontation with Jimmy Truitt. He was ready!

Since the law seemed to be moving at a snail's pace, Ray felt that the incident with the Truitt boy would create a stir and put fire under the Sheriff. It was time to bring those boys to justice, it was time that Raenelle received news that would bring her some peace.

~~~~~~~~

'The son-of-a-bitch had busted his windshield, called him names and made him piss himself.'

Eugene was angry at himself for allowing that man scare him that way. He had run off lie a little weasel. As much as Ray Porter's size intimidated him, Eugene felt that he should have at least made an attempt to fight back or at respond to the man's accusations. Instead he drove away like a coward. He had a switchblade in his glove compartment, he should have used it then. He felt like he had turned into his brother Lester; he acted like a punk. He knew that he was nobody's fool. He slammed on his brakes and the pickup came to an abrupt stop.

"Damn, damn!" He rammed his fist into the dashboard.

His heart raced and the burn on his arm hurt. He took two deep breaths and then got out of the truck; he used an old rag and brushed away the pieces of glass that had landed on the seat. He was so scared after the monster attacked him that he had forgotten that there was shattered glass all over him. Luckily, the cap he wore had protected him shards of glass from hitting him in his head. He examined himself and found that there was no other apparent injury; he knew that once he got home and checked again that he would possibly find some cut or scrape.

Eugene looked at the burn on his arm again; it oozed a yellowish liquid. The idea of going to the clinic vanished from his thoughts. His plans for the day were railroaded by the *scary* episode that just happened outside of the school. He got back into the pickup, put it into gear and headed home. He would apply the same cream he on the burn that he used the previous night; it would have to do for now. There were other things that he needed to take care of.

The next thing on his list was to talk to Lester before the Sheriff got to the house. He decided that he would wait a few minutes at the house and then drive back to meet his brother half way. As he pulled up to the house, he was surprised and disappointed to see his father's and the sheriff's car parked in the yard. Panic rose fast and furious. Eugene knew there would be questions about his hand, the burn was plainly visible. He also knew that his father would certainly question him about the broken windshield of his truck. The hand thing he could explain, and the truck he could think of a lie in a minute. Those were easy questions to answer. What troubled him mostly was the fact that the Sheriff was already there; he was not due to make his visit until later that evening. He wondered what had brought on the sudden change.

Eugene sat in his truck; he needed to think for a minute or two. The day had turned out to be really shitty. First Ray Porter, and now the Sheriff had made an early appearance. There was no way to sneak into the house at that time of day, there was sure to be someone in the kitchen, and if he chose to go through the side door it would mean that he would run into his father or that girl who took Edna's place. Eugene's clothes were wet and messy, his arm hurt and his truck had a started to feel like he had something sharp stuck to his neck and back. He decided to go with what ever came to mind, and if he was approached by anyone when he entered the house; he would handle it. Just as he was about to get out of the truck, he saw his mother's car as it pulled up in the yard.

She slammed the door and ran up to him, all dramatic, clutching her heart.

"Eugene, honey are you alright? What happened to your truck? Did you get in an accident? Oh my God! What happened to your arm Eugene?"

She made an attempt to grab him but he pulled away. Eugene protectively covered his arm.

"It's nothing, I had some radiator blow up on my arm and something flew and crashed into the back of the truck. I'll have my arm looked at and the truck fixed, don't worry about it."

He walked away from her as he spoke; he didn't want any questions regarding the smell of his clothes - that he was in no frame of mind to explain.

"I see the Sheriff is here early." Pearl stated the obvious.

His mother stopped and peeked into the Sheriff's car, whatever was her reason, Eugene did not ask. He wanted to hurry into the house, take a bath and then attend to his hand. He was in no mood for the Sheriff or his parents. However, his mother continued to speak.

"Looks like I may have to go get Lester from school and get this darn thing over and done with once and for all. For the life of me I cannot imagine who would say that you are involved in this whole mess. Edna is like family; she practically raised you boys. What a shame."

Pearl stopped before taking the first steps that led to the porch, she looked at her well-manicured garden. She pulled a few weeds from the midst of the Azaleas, they were blooming beautifully, despite the summer heat. She had kept on talking but it was a one-sided conversation because Eugene had gone around to the side of the house and through the kitchen door.

"Hello Son."

Jimmy Truitt seemed just as surprised to see his son as Eugene was to find his father in the kitchen.

"Hello, I uh, I had to come home to clean up." Eugene responded nervously.

"I'm just going to change and then I'll be right out."

He bolted past his father and headed for his room. He felt the sweat that had formed across his forehead. In the safety of his room, he took off his soiled clothes and heaped them in a pile on the floor. He wrapped himself in a towel, locked his bedroom door and then slipped into the bathroom.

The cool water felt good on his body but made him grimace in pain when it hit his arm. He wanted to wash away any pieces of glass that may have lodged in the nasty burnt flesh. He still needed to find something proper to put on it in the meantime until he could make it to the clinic. It hurt beyond words but he had to suck it up.

The burn on his arm was nothing in comparison to the questions from the Sheriff that he would have to answer. He wished Lester was there but as Eugene thought about it more, it came to him; he had finally figured out the plan. The Sheriff never intended to question them together, he knew that Lester would still be at school at that time of the day and that Eugene would normally be at work. There was no doubt in his mind that Sheriff Whitfield had something up his sleeve. He was glad that he made the decision to go home early.

~~~~~~~~~

Lester fidgeted with the pencil and paper. He had no idea what to write; his mind was blank. The questions that he needed to answer on the test sheet seemed foreign; like he'd never been taught anything about the subject before. He looked at the giant clock on the wall in front of the classroom; thirty more minutes before the bell would ring, thirty more minutes before he would bolt through the door and be on his way home. He decided that come what may, he would tell what happened that night. He couldn't live with the torture of his conscience anymore. Despite the fact that the girl had embarrassed him and that Eugene had threatened to hurt him if he didn't stick to their story of not being involved; He was determined to tell the truth. Lester knew that he needed to clear his conscience. The time had come for him to confess.

The teacher, Miss Blackburn, a short, pudgy, red cheeked woman, walked over to his desk. She had noticed him fiddling around. She saw the blank sheet of paper sitting on his desk and motioned for him to meet her outside the classroom. He pulled his chair back, it scraped against the floor. Other students grumbled but Lester paid them no mind as he followed her out the door.

When they got outside, Miss Blackburn asked him about his blank answer sheet; she told him that she knew he was more than capable of passing the test. Lester shrugged his shoulders, there was no real reason he could think of to give her except that he just wanted to leave school. Miss Blackburn continued to speak. She explained that he should make an attempt to complete even a portion of the test, she further advised that he had more than enough time to do so and begged him to make the attempt. Again Lester just shrugged his shoulders. He didn't care much at this point.

Miss Blackburn shook her head and sighed, she gave Lester permission to return to his seat. When he got back to his desk he decided to mark any answer just so he could finish the test and leave. He ran down the list of questions and checked any letter and within 5 minutes he was done. He collected his books from under the desk, walked up to Miss Blackburn's desk, and handed her the test sheet. She took it but her eyes remained on him; she peered over her too small spectacles. She waved at him, a gesture giving him permission to leave. Lester practically ran out of the classroom; he was anxious to get home.

The afternoon sun blinded him for a minute. The place was quiet and still, there was barely any breeze. When the air did flow, it was hot and heavy. Lester threw his bag over his shoulder and headed toward the gate that led out to the streets. The walk home was not fun; the hike in the heat proved to be a challenge, but Lester needed that time to think; he refused to let the humidity bother him.

He thought about Eugene and wondered how he could be so heartless. He wondered about the power he gave to

Eugene, he had allowed him to control his actions. It had been that way ever since they were boys. Now they were in serious trouble. It seemed like one bad thing after another happened to them; he wondered if they were cursed.

Lester kicked a rock, it skipped for a few yards, and yellowish dust covered his shoes. As he walked on, he thought about what happened *that night*. He felt less of a human, and he had treated the girl – Raenelle – the same way. The image of her beaten body and torn clothes filled his head; they seemed to have found a permanent place in his mind. What right did he have to do that to another human being? What did she ever do to him to deserve that? He was a fool for not standing up and telling his brother that they were wrong, for not stopping the hurt and pain, the senseless actions; he was guilty. He deserved whatever he had coming to him.

He turned to look back at the school; his eyes were moist a mist had come over them. The thought that he may not return there the next day or ever, made his heart heavy. The building slowly disappeared in the distance behind him as he rounded a corner. He took a deep breath and walked on. Today would be *the day*.

~~~~~~~~

The voices of Sheriff Whitfield and his father greeted Lester as he walked through the front door. He removed his bag from his shoulders and placed it on a chair in the living room. He put his books next to it. He wiped his sweaty palms on his pants and walked to the dining area where the adults were. His mother had just refilled the glasses on the table with lemonade.

"Hello Lester."

Pearl put the pitcher on the table next to the men and

then walked over to her son. He appeared somber and the look in his eyes made it seem like his thoughts were a million miles away. She wondered what caused him to be so worried.

"What happened to you Son?"

She patted his shoulders; it was the most affection she'd shown in months. Her touch felt strange.

"Well you should shake that feeling Son. Whatever it is will be over in no time, I'm sure. Now let's just try to relax." She said.

Sheriff Whitfield was taking his sweet time flipping through the pages of his notebook. He next felt around in his pockets in search of a pen.

"I know you want to get this over with Lester, so come on, and let's go clear the air once and for all."

Pearl led her son over to the chair. Lester sat down.

"Go on Son, let's tell the Sheriff that you had nothing to do with anything that has happened around here recently!"

Jimmy Truitt came over and touched Lester's head. This was not the norm; they were not a family that showed that type of emotion or affection. Lester was not sure how to react. so he remained stoic. The Sheriff got up from where he sat; the room seemed to shrink as he came toward Lester. He had his note pad ready, he licked the tip of the pen and got ready to ask questions and to write.

"Relax Son, if the truth is told, there is nothing to be nervous about, ain't that right boy?"

Whitfield shot a glance at Jimmy who nodded in agreement.

"Now tell me Son, did you have anything to do with hurting Raenelle Porter?"

Just as Lester was about to answer, a loud popping sound permeated the homely stillness of the room. Everyone was seriously startled no one knew where the sound came from, but they all watched in confusion and horror as Lester slumped over in the chair. He fell to the floor. In what seemed like slow motion, Pearl sprang over to where her son lay motionless, she dropped on her knees and screamed his name.

Blood flowed onto the pine wood floor as Lester remained still; the Sheriff instinctively drew his revolver and crouched as he surveyed the room. He spotted him! Eugene stood at the doorway between the dining area and the living room. He had a gun pointed in the direction of his family. Pearl continued to scream her youngest son's name, she begged him to wake up. Jimmy yelled at Eugene he pleaded with him to put the gun down.

No one had heard Eugene come into the room, no one heard anything except for the noise the gun made after he had pulled the trigger. Pearl frantically tried to lift Lester's limp body.

"I'm have to take him to the hospital, someone help my son please. Jimmy please, our son is dying."

Jimmy was not sure which direction he should go.

"We've got to get Lester to the hospital NOW!"

She sobbed. Tears streamed down her face. She turned to face her other son.

"Eugene you shot your brother, you shot your brother! What have you done? You shot my baby."

She continued with the sobs.

Eugene watched as his mother struggled to lift his brother. His father was at her side helping. He had grabbed one of Pearl's fancy throws to apply pressure to Lester's wound; the bullet had entered through his son's stomach.

The sight of all the blood and his Lester's lifeless body made Eugene shake. He started to cry uncontrollably but he held fast to the gun; it shook slightly. He never wanted to hurt his brother but he had to. There was no other way.

The Sheriff kept his weapon aimed at Eugene and slowly moved in his direction.

"Don't come any closer Sheriff, I will shoot again".

Eugene used the gun to point the Sheriff in the direction of his parents but the man was determined to move walk to him.

"You don't want to do anything to get into further trouble Son, we can help you. Just put the gun down."

The Sheriff took two more steps towards him; Eugene took two steps back.

Jimmy had picked up his son's limp body and had gone through the door; Pearl grabbed her keys and ran out behind her husband and son; they had to make a life-saving choice.

Their hasty exit somewhat distracted the Sheriff, and Eugene used that opportunity to slip out through the kitchen door. Once outside he ran as fast as he could, he didn't stop until his lungs burned; he panted. The gun was still clutched in his hand. He had no idea where to go, but he knew that he couldn't go back home, he had killed his brother, raped a girl and burned down a house. He started to laugh uncontrollably, and then tears streamed down his face.

Eugene ran a good distance from his house by this time; the Sheriff had not pursued him, not as far as he could *see*. *'Sheriff Whitfield could not run anyway, big fat fool. Who could that big ball go after? What a waste!'* Eugene thought.

He laughed again. He walked on further through the field until he got to the area of some abandoned houses on the other side of town. Ironically it was the same area where they had snatched the girl from that night. He crept up to one of the houses and looked around, there was no one in sight. He pushed the door slowly, the place was musty and dark; he stepped in and closed the door behind him. His arm hurt and his head pounded. He had to collect the many thoughts that swirled in his head.

Everything replayed in his mind. He heard the gun go off, saw his brother slump over; the screams of the girl; he smelled the gasoline he used to start the fire, and he smelled his own flesh burning. He walked around the dark room with gun in hand. He banged his head with his burnt hand ignoring the pain.

"I didn't want him to talk about the things I did. I had to do something. I had to stop Lester from talking. Think Eugene, THINK!"

He realized that he was shouting and instinctively went to look through the window. He couldn't take the risk that someone would find him. By now, the whole neighborhood had probably heard that he had killed his brother.

Darkness began to fall but that would stop nothing everyone would be on the lookout for him. He had to get as far away from Jessup as possible, he needed to leave before the Sheriff found him; before Ray Porter came after him again, and before his mother and father put him in jail because he had killed their precious son. He had to leave Georgia; he had to get away very soon. He decided to be on his way but there was just one last thing that he had to do.

CHAPTER TWENTY-EIGHT

The morning sun streamed through the window as I slowly brushed my hair; the style I had been sporting lately made me look pretty, at least that's what my Daddy had told me. I had taken out the plaits; they looked too *girlie*. I pulled my hair through the elastic band and secured it to the side with a clip. I adjusted the patch over my eye, smoothed out my clothes, then went to get breakfast. It was early enough for me to take my time and enjoy the meal that Grams had prepared. She made biscuits with her special gravy; my favorite. Grams sure knew how to make a girl feel good. Her warm flaky biscuits were always a hit; Daddy would eat six in one sitting. I smiled just picturing him as he patted his belly and told Grams how good a cook she was.

I walked into the kitchen; my place was set and the steaming breakfast waited for me to devour. I expected to see Daddy seated at the table, we always had breakfast together. His usual spot was empty and there was no setting for him. I turned to Grams.

"Where's Daddy?"

"He left early this morning; he went to the Sheriff's office with your mother."

My heart started to race.

"Did something else happen Grams?"

I slumped into the chair; my favorite breakfast didn't look so appetizing anymore. I pushed the plate to the side.

"I'm sure there is nothing for you to worry about Sweetie. Eat your biscuits, they're getting cold. "

Grams busied herself with the dishes, she dried the plate she had just washed; seems like she was making every effort to get every drop of water from the dish. She wiped it over and over. Her actions seemed strange and she had a faraway look in her eyes.

"Grams, is Daddy in trouble?"

I was well aware that my Daddy's temper could make him lose control. He had a way of exploding if the right buttons were pushed. I wondered if he had done something to one of those Truitt boys and had gotten himself arrested.

"You just don't worry about a thing Rae; your Daddy can handle himself just fine."

Grams put the last dish in the cabinet and slowly closed the door.

"Your Daddy wants you to wait for him; he doesn't want you walking to school."

"I know that Grams, I haven't walked to school in a long time."

I unconsciously touched the patch covering my eye. The nightmares had subsided; the scars over other parts of my body were less noticeable. I didn't care much about those things anymore, I just wanted to live my life. My 16th birthday was just around the corner and I had asked my Daddy to take me on a road trip to Virginia, I know that it would be so much fun. He had agreed, and Grams and Momma would go with us, they promised to. The thought of my birthday trip brought my appetite back. I continued to eat my delicious biscuits and gravy; it turned out to be the best yet.

A crashing sound startled both Grams and me; it came from the living room. Grams froze and I spilled the milk from the cup I was holding in my hands. A shadowy figure appeared on the wall; I looked at Grams, she was not sure what to do. My eyes darted back and forth, from Grams to the shadowy figure. My grandmother put her finger on her lips; the signal for me to remain quiet. Grams picked up the rolling pin that lay on the counter. There was heavy breathing and grunting coming towards us. Then Eugene Truitt appeared with a gun in his hand. I spat out the biscuit I just put in my mouth, and Grams lost her grip on the rolling pin.

CHAPTER TWENTY-NINE

Sheriff Whitfield had not called off the search for the Truitt boy, not even when it was way past midnight.

After the boy had escaped from his home, Whitfield checked to make sure that the Truitts had made it to the hospital with their gunshot wounded son. He had gone to his patrol car and radioed his deputy about the situation, giving orders for an imminent search.

The Sheriff's Department started the hunt for Eugene Truitt; he was armed and considered dangerous. The men searched the neighborhood and had gone as far into the woods as the daylight permitted. It was a long shot but the Sheriff thought Eugene may have returned to the scene of the original crime. It was the first place he thought the boy would run to.

The morning after the shooting, the search continued, but there was no real clues about where he could have gone. There visible sign of Eugene. The Sheriff led the deputies in the woods again and doubled back to the Truitt house. He thought that the boy may have returned to get some means of transportation, but his pickup truck remained parked in the same spot, with the back glass shattered. Wherever he was hidden, he had done well to evade them. Whitfield hoped that they would complete the search in the woods and find the boy before sunset.

~~~~~~~~

The Truitts thanked their lucky stars that their younger son was still alive. The bullet had missed major organs. Lester needed to remain intensive care for a while but his prognosis was good. During the chaos and confusion, Jimmy mentioned to the Sheriff that Eugene had used the gun he kept in the house; the boys knew where it was, so for Eugene, it was easily accessible. Jimmy was concerned for his eldest son's life. He wondered what could have driven him to shoot his own flesh and blood. The two were close, Lester adored his older brother. It was incomprehensible.

Pearl's eyes were swollen and puffy; she had cried all night long and there was dried blood all over her clothes. She and Jimmy had remained at the hospital through the night; they wanted to make sure that Lester was ok and comfortable. Since it was morning and their son was stable, they decided to drive home. It was morning time and they were sure that Lester was stable and resting comfortably, they finally drove home. Pearl needed to change before returning to the hospital; that was her intent.

Despite his fatigue, Jimmy wanted to get to his other son. The boy had gotten himself in some serious trouble and as a man of the law, and his father, it was time that he stepped in to help him out. It was a silent ride; there were no words to describe what had happened; Pearl sat with her elbow on the car door handle. She would sigh then sob occasionally. It was a time of confusion. One minute they were sitting in their living room and the next they were clutching their child who had had been shot and almost lost his life at the hands of his own brother.

When arrived at the house, the sight of the huge red stain on the living room floor brought on another flood of tears from Pearl. She asked her husband how their son Eugene could do this to his own brother. She wanted to know what had gotten into him. She was concerned about his whereabouts; she cursed at the state of her life; it was not what she pictured it would be at this stage. Things like this was not supposed to happen to good people like them.

~~~~~~~~

The Sheriff had stopped by the hospital earlier in the morning to let them know that Eugene had not been found. He assured them that he would do his best to find a favorable end to the situation. He was cautious when he reminded them that their son would be treated as any fugitive who was armed and dangerous.

When they arrived home, Jimmy instructed Mahalia to draw a bath for his wife and to make her some tea. When everything was ready Pearl took the tea and then when to lay in the tub of warm sudsy water. Jimmy washed his face, changed his clothes and left. He made sure to tell Mahalia to keep an eye on his wife as he walked through the door. She was in a fragile state. He needed to go find Eugene. He wanted to his son before someone else did.

CHAPTER THIRTY

At the Sheriff's office that morning Ray and Edna listened attentively as Whitfield gave his account of the situation that happened at the Truitt's house the evening before.

Word had already spread that one brother was killed by the other. It was also rumored that Jimmy had had the task of watching the Sheriff lead one of his sons to the precinct lock up. Whitfield had suggested starting the latter to avoid vigilante justice. People were already certain that the boys were responsible for burning of the Johnson's house. The fact that Eugene was carrying what may still be a loaded gun was too dangerous to be made known. Mass chaos was something the town did not need at that time.

Sheriff Whitfield had already called Sheriff Hatch in the nearby town of Hinesville and asked that they remain on standby, just in case the situation got out of control. Whitfield prayed that Eugene would come to his senses and turn himself in. The boy had let once situation go from bad to worse when he decided to aim the gun and put a bullet into his brother.

~~~~~~~~

Ray shifted in his chair. There was need for concern; with this boy on the loose there was no telling what he might was capable of doing. He made things worse for himself by running and hiding. Suddenly it came to Ray, his protective intuition set an alarm off in his head. The fool was out there and his exact location was unknown. Raenelle could be in danger. Ray got up and hurriedly took Edna's arm.

"Let's go Edna" he already had his hat on and his car keys in hand.

Home was where he needed to be, not here. If that *psycho* fool was on the loose with a gun, then his daughter was certainly not safe. There was no time to waste, he needed to get to the house right away!

Edna grabbed her purse and gave the Sheriff a confused look.

"Mr. Porter, I know what you are thinking and I must warn you Sir that vigilante justice is never the way to solve issues such as this. If you or your family is in immediate danger I do expect you to protect them, but I implore you to use common sense in all scenarios."

Ray rushed out of the office without acknowledgement that he had heard the words spoken by Sheriff Whitfield.

CHAPTER THIRTY-ONE

"Get over there you!"

Eugene pointed the gun at Grams, directing her to stand next to me.

"What do you want from us? Haven't you caused enough damage already?"

Grams stood her ground.

"Look old woman, if you want me to use this I will."

Eugene pulled something on the gun; the sound was enough to get Grams to move. I couldn't breathe, I watched as my grandmother made her way over to the table where I stood.

Grams repeated her question.

"What is it that you want boy?"

Eugene looked at his left arm, it was multi colored from wrist to elbow and he was sweating profusely. He looked as if he was about to throw up. Hs skin was pale, his eyes were red and puffy, as if he had not slept all night. It was possible that he had been crying. Then again, a monster such as he had no tears.

Grams eyed the gun, then she looked at the boy again. He had fear was in his eyes and was probably more scared than we were. I felt as if I could read my grandmother's thoughts – I knew what she was thinking; I could tell by the look on her face. She watched me shake as the tears streamed down my cheeks.

"I need to take care of a problem!" He spat the words out.

Eugene blinked a number of times, he looked like he had trouble focusing and he shivered; he had the chills.

"You look sick boy."

Grams kept her tone even, showing fear was not an option at that time. I clung to her arm with the force of an alligator's clamped teeth.

"I'm not sick, *I'M NOT SICK*!"

Eugene started to amplify his voice.

He shook the gun at us.

"Just sit, no stand, just stand there. You come here!"

He pointed at me.

"No No!"

Grams shouted at him as she held on to me and shielded me in a most protective way. She was ready to go in my place.

"I'll do whatever you want just let her be."

Grams held on to the table and started to walk towards him. She fought to release the grip I had on her. He became more agitated, pointed the gun, and then a shot rang out.

CHAPTY THIRTY-TWO

Ray drove his car though the streets of Jessup like a bat out of hell. He needed to get back to the house. His daughter was there, and with that idiot son of a bitch on the loose, there was no telling what could happen. The Sheriff was so casual about the fact that the boy had shot his own brother and was still out there somewhere. He was angered that they could they not find him, and that he wasn't notified as soon as the incident took place. He wondered if there was more that he was not made privy to.

Ray was so deep in thought that he did not hear Edna's pleas for him to slow down. He had gone to the Sheriff's office with the anticipation that he would get news that he long awaited. He wanted to hear that they had enough evidence to charge the two boys with the rape and beating of his daughter, and for burning down the Johnson's home. The piece of nerve-racking news was not what he expected!

He floored the accelerator. He had to hurry, time was of the essence and he could not afford to be one second late. He all but ignored the traffic lights; his anger was building and the fire that he had tried hard to suppress had made its way through his veins. There would be hell to pay if that son-of-a-bitch dared to put his filthy hands on his daughter again.

~~~~~~~~

The night before, Baby Boy and his mother had to leave Jessup and go to North Carolina to live with a relative. Mrs. Johnson had sunk deeper into depression and needed someone else besides her son to care for her. Everyone cried when their cousin came with his truck and packed up the belongings they had left.

That day, I held on to Baby Boy for a long time, I could hardly catch my breath, I cried so much. He assured me that I would be fine, and told me that I should be strong. We would see each other again, he said to me. Through my sobs, I thanked him for saving my life. Even Momma cried. Life without Baby Boy would never be the same, we would miss him so.

~~~~~~~~

As they neared the house, Ray's sixth sense went into high gear; something was amiss. Normally Raenelle would have already heard his car drive up the road and would be on the porch waiting with a big grin on her face. The place was too quiet. Ray parked on the street and told Edna to stay in the car; he put his hands to his lips; a gesture for her to be quiet. He quietly got out of the vehicle and motioned to her that he would be going into the house.

He noticed something strange, the front door was ajar; they never left the door open. Ray looked at Edna, she stared back blankly and shook her head.

Ray crept around to the back of the house, he peered

through the window into Raenelle and Grams' bedroom; there was no movement, no voices coming from that room. He then made his way to the side of the house where the kitchen was located; he heard muffled sounds; soft sobs. It was Raenelle; he knew his daughter's cries.

Ray used stealth moves to make his way up the back steps and to the door. He had to be careful; he was not sure what the situation was behind the walls that separated him from his child. Any sudden moves could be detrimental.

"Please just let Raenelle go!"

Grams' pleas broke through the sobbing.

It was confirmed, Ray's worst fears had come true. He carefully turned the knob on the door, it was locked. Since he knew that the situation was confined to the kitchen area, he decided that it would be better to try entering the house from the front.

Ray had hidden his gun behind some books on a shelf in the living room. From the day he arrived he wanted to put his gun in a safe but close spot. He hustled around the house and just as he rounded the corner he noticed another car parked next to his. It was Jimmy Truitt. Ray was shocked to see the man, he had some balls; he was not wanted around here. Questions ran through Ray's mind. He wondered if the man came to confront him. There was a possibility that he lied about not knowing his son's whereabouts. Ray could handle whatever Jimmy Truitt came to deliver, but the timing was bad – really bad!

CHAPTER THIRTY-THREE

After he left his house, Jimmy drove directly to the service station where his son worked. He was sure that Eugene had gone there to hide. The boy had a messed up mentality, he didn't think about his actions until after he had carried them out. It was a sorry life that he led - a service station attendant – that was all he would ever be.

Lester had the chance of being a star football player; he had skills just like his father; Jimmy shook his head as he thought about his injured son. He hoped that when he recovered that could get back into his games.

He shook his head in disbelief as the entire scene from last evening replayed in his mind. All the boys had to do was answer a few questions from the Sheriff. He would've never guessed in a million years that it would have played out the way it did. However, regardless of who did what, there was a process that had to be followed. Jimmy banged his hand on the steering wheel. Jimmy Truitt, the Warden with a fugitive son, he shook his head at the thought. He would be the laughing stock of the entire town and its environs – the laughing stock of the state! The people who despised him would have more to talk about. Damn that boy!

He pulled up to the service station and walked into the small store, a skinny pimpled face boy looked up from the magazine he was thumbing through and stared.

"Yea?"

That was his greeting.

"I'm looking for Eugene Truitt" Jimmy said matter-of-factly.

"Listen mister, that sorry excuse for a worker has not been here in two days and he never even came to turn in the keys to the garage, he needs to do that. If you know him give him that message."

The boy returned to his magazine.

"I'm his father."

Jimmy glared at the kid, but the young man's expression did not change.

"Well then maybe you can tell him that he is a lazy fool and that he no longer has a job! You tell him that Mister."

Jimmy shook his head then went back outside; he decided to look in the garage. He walked around the building and looked for clues; anything that may point to Eugene's whereabouts; there was nothing obvious so he got back into his car. He drove through the side of Jessup which he barely ever travelled; the area where all the abandoned and boarded buildings were located. He drove slowly through the streets, he got out of his car every now and again to take a closer look inside one building and then another. He looked at the few faces of men and women who had made the streets their home; none was Eugene. The boy could not have gotten far, his truck was still parked at the house. If he had taken the bus in an effort to get out of town at any time that morning, Jimmy he would have been known. He continued his search, he had to keep looking, and he had to find his son.

One of Jimmy's correctional officers radioed to alert him that had heard the Sheriff's department search was continuing at a frenzied pace. The officer confirmed that there had been no sightings up to that point. Jimmy was also informed that the Sheriff had alerted all of his personnel: on-duty and off-duty, regular and volunteer: to be on the lookout for the boy. He shuddered when he heard that the Sheriff had reminded his men that Eugene was armed and considered dangerous.

Jimmy continued to drive around the streets of Jessup. He even drove through the central part of town, but there was still no sight of his older son. Time ticked by and he began to get discouraged; he desperately needed to find Eugene. He wondered about his younger son's condition and about his wife.

He wondered would talk to the Sheriff about the shooting, after all Lester would be just fine; it had to have been an accident; that was the only logical explanation. It was due to the pressures of being accused of hurting that girl, the nerve of Sheriff Whitfield. How dare he think that Jimmy Truitt's sons could commit such an act?

Jimmy's thought about Ray Porter and his boldness; he dared to show up at the house and make allegations and threats. It was the fault of both men that one son was on the run and the other was laid up in a hospital. He needed to show Ray Porter what it felt like to be threatened in his own place, he needed to show Ray Porter that he was not afraid of him, as big as he was. Ray Porter needed to know that Jimmy Truitt was no coward. He turned his car onto the road that would take him to Edna's house.

~~~~~~~~

Sheriff Whitfield received the morning check-in reports from the bus terminal and train stations, but they had come up empty. None of the men that he had sent to guard these ports had seen anyone fitting Eugene's description. A drive by his house confirmed that his pickup truck was still parked in the same spot. The boy had disappeared during the night. They would have to do a very thorough search that day. The Sheriff from Hinesville had sent 4 of his deputies to assist and they were ready to go.

The Sheriff gave his usual speech about the preservation of life and about the use of deadly force as the last resort. No-one was to fire their weapon until he gave the order for them to do so or if they were in undoubted fear for their own lives. He briefed them all on the situation and how they were to keep in close contact with him. The men then filed out of the station to their respective vehicles and headed to various locations around town. They patrolled the streets, stopped and searched abandoned buildings and asked questions of citizens; no-one could remember seeing the boy. Sheriff Whitfield then decided to drive by the Porter house. He would get the chance to check on her and see if she could answer some questions in the mean time. He would also make sure that Ray Porter had not gone out on his own manhunt as well. He directed one of the patrol cars to follow him.

As he neared the house, he recognized Jimmy Truitt's car.

He wondered what the man was doing at that location.

Sheriff Whitfield slowed his patrol vehicle, the other car matched his move. There had to be trouble. What else would bring Jimmy Truitt to this side of town?

CHAPTER THIRTY-FOUR

Eugene slid down the kitchen wall, he shook more now; sweat ran down his face; he felt hot then cold and the chills made his body tremble uncontrollably. The pain from his burnt arm was so intense that he felt he would pass out. The shot he had fired earlier had hit a cabinet in the kitchen that housed drinking glasses. The door had shattered and glasses dropped to the table, floor, and on the old woman. A broken piece fell on her head, she got a gash on her head that bled more than anything he had ever seen. The blood made the girl scream; she wouldn't stop screaming. He yelled at her to shut up but she screamed even louder. Finally he told her that if she didn't shut up the next bullet would go straight into the old woman's heart. That was enough to quiet her.

Eugene wanted something for the pain. He couldn't tell which was more intense, the pain in his head or the pain from his oozing burnt arm. He told the girl to get a kitchen towel from the counter for the bleeding woman; then they were all to move to the medicine cabinet in search of something for his pain. Sweat dripped into his eyes and the saltiness stung. He ushered the girl and her grandmother into the bathroom area, told the girl to grab a bottle of pills, and then pointed them back to the kitchen. The girl opened the bottle and the pills spilled onto the table, Eugene grabbed four of them, they scraped his throat as he swallowed. He would wait for the pain to subside, then decide upon his next move. He had to get out of town, the girl would be his ticket, and the old lady was a bonus.

~~~~~~~~

Ray hurried to Jimmy Truitt's car.

"What the hell are you doing here?" He asked angrily.

Ray's rage was visible.

"Did you come to join your son? Did you send him here to finish what he started? What kind of monsters have you raised?"

Jimmy clenched his jaw; the words coming from Ray's mouth were accusatory and they insulted him. What did he mean join his son?

"Do you have my son hostage in your house?"

Jimmy made an effort to get out of the car but Ray stopped him when he shoved the door shut. He leaned in further and was within inches of Jimmy's face.

"Your son is in that house with my daughter! Why did you come here? Did you know he would be here?" Ray wanted to punch Jimmy Truitt in the face.

Ray's anger rose by the second; he had no time to waste he had done enough talking to the man. He needed to get into the house and rescue his daughter.

"Listen mister, your son has a gun, you very well know that." Ray pointed to his home.

"I have no idea what you are talking about Mr. Porter. Why would I send my son here? What are you saying?" Jimmy was confused.

Sheriff Whitfield drove up; he exited his vehicle and rushed up to the men. They looked like they were in the middle of a very heated argument.

"Good day gentlemen, what seems to be the trouble?"

He adjusted his suspenders.

"Listen Sheriff that crazy kid is in the house with my daughter. I need to get her and her grandmother out and they'd better be unharmed. Whatever happens to that Truitt fool is none of my concern."

Ray spat the words out and made a move to head into the house, the Sheriff held him back. He could tell that the man was agitated.

"Are you sure you saw Eugene?" The Sheriff wanted to confirm Ray's accusations somehow.

Ray angrily shrugged off the Sheriff's grip. How dare he ask him such a question? They wasted enough time, he did not want to talk when they should be in the house saving his daughter. Whitfield decided to take charge of the situation.

"Listen Mr. Porter, I understand that you want to get your girl, but the risk you may be taking by barging in is great. If you startle him or go in unprepared, you may be sorry. The kid was last seen with a gun; he may still have it. Have you seen your daughter? What happened when you got here?"

Jimmy was curious to hear the response to the questions.

Ray told Sheriff Whitfield what he had heard in the kitchen. Then the Sheriff signaled to his two deputies in the other patrol car. They came over and after being briefed they were directed to the back of the house with their weapons drawn and ready; he reminded them to wait for his 'go' before they made a move to apprehend.

~~~~~~~~

Edna sat in the car the entire time. She saw the patrol cars, Jimmy Truitt, Ray; she sat transfixed. She watched as the two deputies walked around to the back of her house; she watched as the Sheriff, gun in hand, walked up the steps that led to her living room. Ray and Jimmy Truitt had walked into the house behind the Sheriff. Fear gripped her as she willed her hands to open the car door, and then her legs to move. She got out of the car and waited.

After three minutes or so she heard screams, shouts and other noises she could not identify. She watched as Ray emerged from the house with their daughter in his arms; she saw the Sheriff lead her mother out of the house behind Ray and Raenelle. There was no sign of Jimmy Truitt, for some reason unknown to her he had stayed inside. She fell to her knees when she saw the blood soaked towel around her mother's head.

Minutes Prior

The two deputies had gone around the back of the house to cover the kitchen exit while Sheriff Whitfield went through the front. Loud sobs came from the rear of the house, and there was heavy breathing; it sounded like someone was pacing back and forth.

"Listen I'm getting out of here one way or another, I just need to think."

It was Eugene's voice; one of the deputies recognized it. He signaled to the other deputy to be quiet. They would wait to hear if the Sheriff had gotten inside, his signal would clear them to move in.

The Sheriff moved slowly in the direction of the voice he heard, he stopped and looked over his shoulder; Ray Porter and Jimmy Truitt had entered the house right behind him. The Sheriff signaled at both men to be quiet. He whispered a caution to them warning that they could complicate matters if their presence was sensed. Then he moved further into the room until he had Eugene in his sight. The boy stood next to the small gas stove, he looked terrible: ashen complexion, sunken eyes, sweaty and trembling. He still had the gun.

He shook as he spoke.

"This is your fault entirely you little bitch. Why didn't you just die that night? Why! Why didn't you die?"

He lifted the gun. It was the wrong move. The deputies busted through the back door and the Sheriff rushed into the room. In a split second he took a quick scan around the room. The two females were crouched together by the table, the younger one started to scream. The older woman looked too injured to get up or to speak, she had a blood soaked rag wrapped around her head, and she needed medical assistance.

"Drop the gun Son!"

Sheriff Whitfield signaled to the deputies to hold their fire.

"I'll shoot them both, I swear I will. Nobody come any closer."

The boy looked like he would pass out at any moment. Ray Porter made his way to the commotion; he had a gun pointed at Eugene – he aimed for that spot between his eyes.

The Sheriff spoke to him next.

"You don't want to do anything foolish now do you Mr. Porter? We have it under control sir, please put down your weapon."

Whitfield kept his eyes on Eugene; the deputies kept their eyes and guns on Ray. When he realized that he was cornered, Eugene pointed the gun at the girl and yelled at them all to get back, tears streamed down his face; he drooled as he spoke.

"I'm not going to jail, I'd rather kill myself first, and she is the cause of all of this!"

"No son, we can talk about it."

Whitfield tried to calm the boy, he needed help. It was obvious.

"I shot my brother because of her. I shot my brother and now he's dead!"

"Come on Son, just give me the gun; the Sheriff inched

closer, Ray and Jimmy followed.

"Don't come any closer!" Eugene yelled.

"Just give me the gun son; it doesn't have to end this way. Your brother is fine; he's going to make it."

"Two more steps closer and I'm doing it. You're a liar! He's dead! I saw him lying on the floor with all that blood!"

Ray Porter had had just enough of this talking. The boy all but admitted to hurting his baby girl.

"Just drop the damned gun!"

Ray shouted at Eugene; he thought that the Sheriff was being too nice.

Confused and dizzy, frightened, shaking, and in pain – so much pain, Eugene looked at Ray, then at the Sheriff. He returned his focus on the girl. It was time to pull the trigger.

There was a sudden darkness as he felt his own body falling to the floor. The faces of his mother, brother and father flashed before him; he gasped for air, but instead a gurgling sound fell from his lips, followed by, "Dad". He felt the *pains* finally subside as life exited his body he took his last breath.

Jimmy Truitt – the Warden – had brought one of his handguns; he had shot and killed his own son!

CHAPTER THIRTY-FIVE

I could not wait to hit the road.

"Virginia here I come."

I smiled at the thought of taking that long drive in my Daddy's car. The ride would last for hours he had explained; it did not bother me one bit. I had never been on any trip before, but my Daddy had shared stories of his experiences with me on many occasions and it all seemed to be fun. A new and beautiful life awaited me. I was anxious to leave this place and all the bad memories behind. I would miss my friend Ruthie, we had said our goodbyes and promised to write each other. It was a bittersweet moment.

I watched as Daddy put the last of the bags in the car. The bulky stuff had already been transported out by truck a few days ago. It was a week after Daddy and Momma got married at Pastor Wilson's church. The wedding was small, only six people – including my parents. It was beautiful.

Momma stood watching the empty house, it was as if she wanted to take it with us. Grams was well seated in the back of the car waiting for Momma to join her. She seemed more anxious than me to leave.

"Come on y'all let's get going"

Grams voice was filled with joy as she called out to my parents, but no one was happier to get into the car than me. It was finally happening, the glorious beginning of a new life.

Five months later:

"Good Morning Warden", your newspaper is waiting for you Sir, as well as a steaming pot of Coffee.

"Good Morning and thank you Angela."

"How are Earl and the kids?"

"They're just fine Sir, they're all doing well."

Jimmy Truitt had just arrived at work. The past few months were tough – mentally and emotionally he was drained – but he coped as best he could. Eugene's funeral was a sad and burdensome affair, but Jimmy was relieved to have it over and done with.

He was cleared by a psychologist, and had returned to work after one month's bereavement time-off. Today he was anxious to call and get a weekly update from the juvenile detention facility in town. One inmate was of great interest. That same inmate had also tried to kill himself a month ago. His name was Lester Truitt; he would remain under suicide watch for the duration of his stay.

Lester had recovered from his gunshot wound, and was sentenced to serve time at the juvenile facility; he was still 17 years old. When he turned 20, he would be transferred to the Prison where his father was the Warden, to complete a 10 year sentence.

Jimmy hung up the phone after getting a satisfactory update from the juvenile facility. He leaned back in his chair and heaved a huge sigh. He now had another call to make; another update to get; this time from the town's Psychiatric Center. His wife – Pearl – was warded there.

J. Carie-Ann Burton

About the Author

J. Carie-Ann Burton was born in Antigua. After completing her secondary education, she migrated to the United States; she now resides in New Jersey. She holds a Masters Degree in Business Administration, a Bachelors Degree in Health Administration with a concentration in Health Management and an Associate's Degree in Elementary Education. She is currently a Financial Analyst in the healthcare industry.

Contact with J. Carie-Ann can be made through email at jcarieann@gmail.com